Wen

Wilson

Wen

Wilson

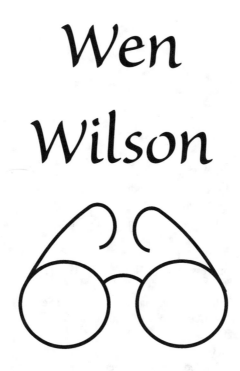

Mattie McClane

SECOND EDITION

Copyright © 2009, 2022
Myrtle Hedge Press, Kure Beach, North Carolina

ISBN 978-1-7329970-1-1
Library of Congress Control Number 2021950117

Design by Val Sherer, Personalized Publishing Services
Photo 41910269 © Paulbuhr | Dreamstime.com

To Dale Billingsley

Contents

Preface

It has been said, "Nothing happens by accident in politics." It could also be said that no dystopian novel happens by accident either: an author summons the real shadowy or partially hidden political forces, and the imagination gives it life. *Wen Wilson* is such a tale. It is the story of a writer/activist who is caught up in America's transition from a democratic republic to a totalitarian regime.

Wen Wilson is a known agitator because of his writings. The powers-that-be do not understand how he knows what he knows; they have actively suppressed his writings and banned the publication of future books. They attempt to silence him. They hound him, driving him from city to city, so he finds no rest. He stops at Dan-U Farms.

Wen Wilson is set in Missouri, in a small midwestern town. Ruth Uppers assumes the ownership of an expansive cattle farm after the death of her husband. She is in charge of the operation and oversees its hired help. She acts as the elderly heroine who gives the politically-charged writer refuge on her farm and eventually comes to accept him as almost a family member. Initially, she gives him a job as a farmhand. Later, she would give him space to write.

Wen's residence on the farm sets off the hired hands. They recognize that the newcomer is a targeted man. Not only is he of particular interest to the authorities, he is a bookish man. He doesn't play cards at the men's house or watch television; he reads in his spare time. He is so different, and thus he is a source of suspicion to the other men. One worker mocks him at first with a playful song until the tension becomes too much and results in violence. *Wen Wilson* becomes a study in class relations; it depicts contemporary contempt for what is considered elite.

Yet, Wen's problems extend to a more educated class as well. The community reacts with fear at the prospect of having a noted agitator around. They too are unaccepting of the newcomer.

Repeatedly, they warn Ruth that her bookish hire is trouble. They want Wen Wilson to leave.

The warnings increase when Wen marries a local woman with a child and the family moves into the main farmhouse. The people see that Wen Wilson is now a part of their life sphere and may not simply go away. Wen Wilson and the democracy he stands for become under attack. Ruth Uppers becomes Wen's defender, and she uses her resources to protect him.

Ruth Uppers has been called "a memorable character." Ruth is a pragmatic librarian, turned farmwoman. She is a solid citizen who both leads and serves the people around her. She is acutely aware of her position as a female boss in charge of younger, more physical men. She is an equestrian and a sure-shot with a pistol. She is loyal to Wen and his family even while they are abused.

Wen Wilson was first written in 2005, first published in 2009. I was a political columnist in 2005. Before then, I was active in leadership roles in the League of Women Voters. The League taught me a lot about democracy, so I could see when its principles were being subverted. The seemingly prophetic book was born from my imagining a worst-case scenario after G W. Bush's years.

George W. Bush's era planted the seeds of an America now on the verge of authoritarianism. Partisanship marked the times. There was a growing intolerance of differences. Incivility was rising. The fossil fuel industry took a seat at the White House table. Dick Cheney famously hosted several unnamed energy companies on site; the meeting was used to set oil policies.

That Iraq possessed WMDS was an obvious lie, maybe the first lie of many future lies so big as to corrupt a country. Iraq's War was perpetrated to divide Hussein's oil fields among nations. High officials promoted falsehood in an increasingly partisan nation. Oil companies had a grip on the country that has only tightened over the years. Today fossil fuel companies, the primary funder of the Republican Party, through their minions, are the biggest threat to our democratic tradition.

Trump's administration neglected the United States' traditional allies or NATO in favor of oil rich countries, Russia and Saudi Arabia. I suspect that global fossil fuel interests are responsible for growing disinformation and a boardroom aim for an American authoritarian government. A democratic republic would far more willingly face and attempt to fix the planet's climate crisis.

It is ironic that *Wen Wilson's* opening scene shows the all too common deluge and the land flooding so badly that the cattle need to be driven up to higher ground. The incessant rainfall is clearly a sign of climate change, affecting the world.

The 2nd edition's text is original, allowing both for a few inconsistencies and for page-turning suspense. Its prescient vision merits leaving the first version intact. It is an imperfect novel, yet I believe there is much to think about between its covers, about our country, about democracy in America.

Mattie McClane
Wilmington, North Carolina
November, 2021

A Bookish Man

Ruth Uppers circled the table, serving eggs to her farmhands. She hired three since her husband had died; Galliwag was a middle-aged man responsible for a family. Mix had been with the Uppers for years and was approaching 70 years old. David Paul was in his early 20s and never took to school, preferring to stay home when much of his class went away to college.

"We'll move the herd to higher ground, drive it into the woods," said Mix, while cutting an egg with a fork. Seated hired hands nodded at his suggestion but said nothing. Rain had been coming down for two weeks, had saturated the ground, and had nowhere to go except over the top of pasture. The cows looked miserable, as if each had been pulled from the spin cycle of a washing machine. Ruth finally leaned against the counter and listened to the steady pour. These men were necessary, and yet they did not think much of a woman's opinion. It was difficult to be the boss and the morning waitress as well.

She walked to the side porch; it sounded as if the dogs needed to come in. Midget and Harry slept on the porch's painted boards in bad weather. Harry appeared to be jumping at the screen. A man stood in the deluge. He wore a green jacket, made darker, blackish from being wet through and through. He handed Ruth his driver's license as if she were the law. The name was Wendell Wilson. Rain streamed a path down the brim of his hat. He was probably 40.

"Am I supposed to know you? Here, step in from the weather. The name Wendell Wilson means nothing to me." She brought him into the kitchen, so the stranger would know that she was not alone; her old rifle figured prominently against the low cabinets. She vowed that she would not hesitate to use it, but really having it in plain sight was a deterrent.

The man stood in front of the kitchen table, and the hands were showing interest in the stranger. Strangers were rare in Alcott County. He opened his backpack and removed a picture and presented it to Ruth. The hired hands now followed his every move. "My mother was Adda Wilson." Ruth smiled at the photograph, showing her youthful red hair and her friend in college. "I was passing through, and the rain stalled out my car," he said.

Galliwag looked interested. "Water under the distributor cap." The others nodded. "We'll get your car and bring it up."

Wendell Wilson ran his hand through his thick hair. "It's just past the bridge."

Mix stood. "Give us your keys and you can stay here and dry out. It's a walk from the bridge." The hands moved their chairs back against the table, took their coats, and pulled up their hoods. They moved together, seemed to think together, and always had the solution. They mumbled and went out the side door. Ruth went to clean up the dishes.

"I was sad when your mother died," Ruth said. "Tell me, do you carry pictures for any occasion?" You didn't know your car would quit and yet it is like you would have stopped anyway. Do you have business with me, Wendell?" Wen Wilson wiped off his eyeglasses with a napkin from the table and put them on. Their small wire rims made him appear as a stranger, as if a professor had come deep into cattle country; he looked sorely out of place.

"How can I help you?"

"My mother said that you would help me," he said. "You were her friend." Ruth smiled.

"Do you need money? You've come a long way if you need money," Ruth said. "I'm not accustomed to giving money to people who arrive on my doorstep. Now, if you want a job, you can see I have as many men as I need, sometimes they are too many. The way I see it, they left me with a stranger—kind fellows, but sometimes not smart. Would you mind emptying the contents of that bag?" Ruth pointed to it. Wendell looked up to her, was silent, and then slowly opened the bag's drawstrings. One after another, he removed books; some were as worn as discards at a library. Ruth took one book from the pile, John Stuart Mill's *On Liberty*. She was more afraid of him, of this intellectual who had made a long journey to see her.

"I don't need money and for now I don't need a job. I want to stay here for a few days."

He nervously rubbed his fingers.

"Are you in trouble with the law? I want no part of that no matter whose son you are."

"It is beyond me why you came here. Oh sure, your mother; we were friends, good friends, but I won't walk out on a limb for you. I have a good name in this community. Sorry, I can't do it."

"You were a librarian when you lived in St. Louis. You must value freedom, that texts should be free from censorship."

"Whoa, mister, this is cattle country. Life is simple. People do the best to feed their families, pray for the servicemen overseas; they work for a living and would send you a packing with words like 'intellectual freedom.'" Now it came back to her. "Adda said she had a son who was a political writer. She worried about you, thought you were a bit of a renegade. Lord, Lord, now you've come to me; why, because I was a city librarian?"

"You love books," Wendell smiled. "And I would also have to guess that you love order, everything in its place. I eventually want to get a job here, not with you, necessarily, but in the county. I seem out of place to you. But my mother's roots are in this county—and her childhood memories. Those have been passed on. I know a lot about you through the stories that she told. I know about Carrie Jenkins and how she arrived at church late with her six children. She drove a truck with no muffler and raised chickens that were sometimes kicked by the mules." He paused "I *am* a political writer; we now live in a time of widespread censorship. Cultural agents seek to limit my work, hassle me through the IRS."

"You can't stay. Cultural agents, whoever heard of such a thing?"

"They monitor writing."

He walked to the window, looking for the hired hands and his car. Ruth needed to explain to him more about where he was. Oh sure, he'd heard stories about Alcott County, but this was not New York where men openly cared about public affairs. The residents went to a school board meeting, protested racy contents of old or new books, but people were not political here; they did not stand for causes other than reducing the speed on the bad curve of highway 62.

"Looks like they can't get it started," he said. The farm truck was at the top of the drive.

"Take off those glasses. I don't care if you can see or not, I won't have you looking like a visiting scholar. Put away those books. You don't fit here, can never fit here. Ideas are secondary to cows," Ruth said. Springs on the porch door sounded, and Mix came into the kitchen shaking his head.

"Need to order you a part," David Paul was quick to deliver the bad news.

"Just sputtered and sputtered," Mix added. Galliwag offered to tow the car through the farm gates to get it off the hard road. Ruth looked at Wen, like he had turned the cosmic universe in his own favor. "It will just take a couple of days for the parts to come in. I can call them in on the phone." Mix walked to a wall phone. Ruth wondered about the cattle in the low pasture.

"Drive the cattle to the higher ground. Last thing I need is to have those animals caught in a field flood," she walked by the rifle and touched the top of its barrel. Ruth walked Wen's bag to a chair in the living room. A letter dropped on the floor. She picked it up and held it in her hand until she set it on the kitchen counter. Lazy confusion filled the room.

"Tow the car?" Galliwag awaited orders.

"Yes, yes," Ruth answered with agitation. "But first put the herd on high ground." She went to a closet and removed a pair of rubber boots, the kind that laced up to the middle of the leg. "Get Harry and Midget, will send them to one side of the herd and drive the other side with the truck." She motioned for the hands to get a move on. She looked at Wen, who was nowhere close to dry. "Come on, Elijah Lovejoy," she said to him. "You claim to know a lot about this land. Get in the back of the pickup with David Paul. Let's see if you can move a herd up into the woods."

The hired hands were dumbfounded by Ruth's sudden passion. She really wanted to move those cows. The truck jostled up the muddy road to the middle pasture. Ruth thought about her learned visitor riding in the bed with David Paul and the dogs. Mix drove the truck, and she was seated next to Galliwag. The herd was beginning to come into sight; three cows now noticed the vehicle. "Here, Mix," Ruth said. Mix stopped the truck, and the dogs jumped over the truck bed's walls. They began barking, scurrying in circles, moving the stray animals forward.

Mix began to drive, the tires spun, throwing mud as if from fountains. The herd was clearly in sight and so was the high timber. What was she going to do with Wen for three days until his car parts came in? Everyone knew that getting parts for a car was one of the slowest proceedings in the county. Ruth's mind went back to Adda—what did their friendship mean if indeed she had told him that she would help the rebel son? It wasn't clear what he wanted, rest, refuge, a conversation about the history of the county. Ruth was aware of the musky scent of Mix's bath soap. She looked down and saw red clay on Galliwag's pant leg. She rolled down the window. "You guys okay back there?"

David Paul spit tobacco. "The herd is in the timber," he said, wiping rain from his face. The truck rocked back and forth so that Wen and

David Paul needed to hold onto its sides. Ruth closed the window and instructed Mix to go back to the house without the dogs. They'd bark and yip a bit but would complete the drive and would come back on their own. She supposed that the hands could tow Wen's car through the farm gates if for no other reason than the car did not need to call attention to itself.

The truck stopped at the house. David Paul jumped out, Wen followed, and then the cab emptied. Ruth was relieved that the herd was safe. She was preoccupied by the visitor, and didn't much notice who trailed behind her to the house. She looked back at them, and they were off to tow Wen's car, and were after a heavy chain from the barn. Ruth opened the porch door, he could sleep on the outdoor furniture; the couch looked comfortable, but only Midget and Harry knew for sure. Ruth turned the key of a deadbolt and let herself in.

She went to the counter and picked up the letter: the post might shed some light on Adda's son and his dealings. Ruth eyes ran down the handwritten epistle until they came to underlined words, "I feel certain that you can trust Ruth; she is that kind and is an activist from the 1930s and 1940s when so much was written about book burning and censorship. It is natural for librarians to be on the side of openness; they spend their lives developing meaningful archives." Adda's words made her pause, question who she was. She was a cattle farmer.

Ruth almost folded the letter to put it back. The letter presented a challenge to her. She had arthritis in her left shoulder and didn't need any noble burdens or reminders of the past. Was Ruth a champion of intellectual freedom? The idea was too lofty, the calling was too sublime. The intrigue did not excite her but made her more nervous than she been in years. But "trust" always touched her in a way that few other words could. She had always been trustworthy, always dependable, paid her bills on time, and sat in the same pew on Sundays. People trusted Ruth Uppers, and she was flattered that an old friend had recognized that quality in her. Her mind wandered into the past, to the Communists who tried to hold meetings at the city library. She did not throw them out despite their pacifist agenda.

Many people maintained that they were separate, had forfeited their rights as Americans. Ruth recalled that she felt that they were young people, frustrated with few options in a chaotic world. It was for youth to seek out alternatives and for aged citizens to demand the status quo. Wen Wilson was not a young man, he'd passed the proverbial "age of discontent." In the world that was now Ruth's world, he should be seeing a child off to college or planning for a retirement. Ruth viewed it as a luxury to be so introspective, to imagine that one could change the powers-that-be.

She watched the car as it was towed passed the gates and along the long lane. Ruth noted that Wen's wardrobe hung on hangers across the back-seat of the automobile. Ruth called out to Mix to bring in the clothing. Wen exited the truck and re-moved the pressed shirts and trousers and began to bring them into the house. Ruth had decided to keep Wen on as another hand. She wasn't sure if he could do anything, whether he'd be any help at all around the farm. "Hang those up in the spare room's closet. You won't be wearing them much." She told Mix to drive Wen into town and to pick him out work clothes, no more ironed shirts. Ruth wondered what she was doing. Adda apparently believed in this son and in Ruth. Adda had found the right button and knew that Ruth could never turn down a duty.

Her mind went back to the 1930s, the library steps. A police officer was handcuffing a demon-strator. Ruth remembered watching metal grasp the wrists. Pain was inflicted if a protester tried to turn his hands. A crowd assembled from the street to the library doors. Men wore long over-coats, rumpled from days of constant wear. A woman shaved her head to present a masculine appearance. Loose orange pamphlets fluttered in a wind, stopping, resting, then onto the next square of wide step. People used the steps as a type of outdoor seating. Ruth made her way through thoughtful humanity that morning. Each dem-onstrator was caught in a moment of history, in an event that tenured scholars would write about. A police wagon pulled through the bystanders on the street. People began to move, aimlessly, or seemingly unsure of what would be their next move; some people stood and walked down the steps. Some people began to chant, "Brothers, bring us peace."

Wen was seated at the kitchen table, now re-lieved by Ruth's acceptance. Ruth removed hair-cutting shears from the highest kitchen cabinet. She boldly grabbed at Wen's thick curls, black with strands of gray in places. She turned on the shears and began her work. She'd have no foppish-styled hand. His hair would be cut short, he'd wear work clothes, and his books would be put away. He needed new eyeglasses, no wire rims. Wen would tend cows like the rest of the men. He'd go to church with her on Sundays, but they would not necessarily sit in the same pew or even the same section of the church. He would speak like a common man, a man with no college in his background. Ruth reviewed her terms as she watched Wen's hair come off in waves. Perhaps one day they would talk about the idea of intellectual freedom, but Ruth's actual goal was to show the lofty rebel that the stuff that counted in life were the things that one could touch, abstractions were for useless idealists and philosophers. She wondered what he wrote, what kind of ideas drew out cultural agents. Ruth's curiosity was deep, burning, but she also had a hunch about this man.

He carried books into a former librarian's home, dense, heady texts. Wen Wilson was a literary man. Yet, he paid too much attention to politics, and when it started getting out of control, he was caught up in it. Ruth knew that the country was different now, but she gave the matter almost no attention. The practical woman found cows less complex and would not contemplate "the inalienable rights of man." Mix smiled at Wen's shaved head. "Buy him work clothes," Ruth said. Wen felt his head, looked down at the mess of clippings on the floor.

By evening, Ruth had explained to Wen that he'd be joining the rest of the hired help in the men's house. It was the original farmhouse on the land and had been renovated to house four workers. He was welcomed to come to breakfast, but, for the most part, the hands were on their own for other meals. She showed him his books, still in the living room. "Books really have no place for employees on a working farm, but you may keep them for your free time."

Wen smiled, grateful, more assured. "What made you change your mind?" he asked.

"I'm doing you no favors beyond putting a roof over your head, and you will earn that everyday. I don't want to know about what you write or who you write it for. There'll not be much occasion for philosophical speculation here. We run four herds and your duties will be considerable. I personally will keep you busy, and if you want to talk about the collective conscious after that, fine. But I suspect you'll be hankering for a meal and then rest." Ruth knew that he didn't understand her sudden sympathy, but she did not care. She had tucked Adda's letter between the pages of one of his books. She handed him the bag and told him the men's house would be the lighted building beyond the hill. Ruth knew that he wanted to thank her. Still, she was in no mood for that now.

When Wen tried to make eye contact with her, she turned away as if she was still busy at one more thing.

"Goodnight," Wen said. The door shut. He was gone. Ruth predicted that it would take her a while to fall asleep. She took a hot bath, soaking her body, trying to rid it of its chill from cold rain. She dried off and took her terrycloth robe from the hook at the back of the door. In her bare feet, she walked across hardwood floors and opened a pair of creaky pocket doors. Inside, the room was an expansive library. The shelves had been built by her late husband to make a place for all the discards Ruth had retrieved from the trash bins. She rested on a sofa and was surrounded by books of every color; the words of sages, of storytellers, of politicians, of historians. The books were like ghosts from a former life. There was a woman who saved books; it sounded like the beginning of a nursery rhyme. She had not entered this room for more than a year. Ruth stood to check the dust that had accumulated on the shelves' surfaces. The room had been neglected, in part, because it brought back memories of her marriage and dead son and because she wasn't sure what the past meant. Did she still believe that it was worth preserving, detailing, and chronicling for future generations? She imagined herself to be an extinct animal encircled by years of knowledge. Did the knowledge stop the earth's warming trend? Did community leaders vigorously heed scientific findings? The best books of the collection were kids' stories. A mother's voice had spoken the words out loud with the hope of enjoyment. Ruth felt relieved, having revisited the library with all its haunts. She addressed God in the silence. "Lord, I don't know why this nonconformist has come my way. It will help me if you remember that I'm a woman who has now gone beyond her prime. I move much slower than in prior days. This man, Adda Wilson's son, knows me no better than anyone off the street, and yet he has touched me with his passion or maybe desperation. I am going to try, but Lord, sweet Jesus; I doubt my power to stop a thinker from thinking, to stop his leanings. I have dressed him like a Missouri farmer. And tomorrow I'll send him to the apple orchard with a ladder. He has seen the farm, but only you have seen this room. Are you inclined to lead him here, because I was so set against him at the first, and I'm softening, losing resistance, feeling a kinship with his love of books? I am in this room." She pressed her fingers against a Bible, but did not take it down. Then she turned and hit the light switch. She went to her bedroom. Ruth Uppers unfolded her bed covers and slept soundly through the night's rain.

Morning's sunshine filled everyone with energy. Galliwag was balancing a spoon on the top of his hand. Ruth looked out her window and saw David Paul practicing kicking a football. Mix would hold it, and David Paul showed off his unusual form. Wen stood by, was an interested onlooker. Galliwag joined Ruth at the window. "Look at Wilson's shoes," he instructed Ruth. "That man's a city slicker of some kind. A man can't work in shoes like that." Ruth noted the heavy gloss on leather. Ruth's attempt to wardrobe Wen had fallen short. Mix was putting ladders on the truck and was planning on going to the orchard. Galliwag was right; Wen would slip with such smooth soles. He would not be able to stay on a ladder. "Mix says he reads way into the night, doesn't have a lot to say about where he's from. I'll be glad when his car part comes in and we can wish him on"

Ruth dried her hands, wiping off suds from the dishwater. "Galliwag, I've hired him. He's going to be around. As for his shoes, I imagine that they are church shoes or for a special occasion.

He's as regular as the next guy. Why bankers and businessmen don't take work on cattle farms. He seems to have as little money in his pocket as the next guy." Ruth paused, assessed Galliwag's shock at Wen having a permanent job on the farm.

"Mrs. Ruth, you don't know the guy. I hear about these slick fellows who take older folks for their money. They're confidence men, say the right words, have a gentleman's ways, but are up to no good."

Ruth raised one arm as if to dismiss the idea. "Thanks Galliwag, but Wen Wilson isn't going to be packing a farm into his book bag. Goodness, we shouldn't be judging him because of a fine pair of shoes. He's not much of a farmer, his grandfather was a farmer. I know that for a fact. Galliwag, he's an educated man. His mother, my friend, made sure he took to studies. So if he doesn't seem like the perfect farm help, he isn't, I mean if we're counting days in the field. But give him time, he'll come around and be very useful."

"Lotta strong hands would like to get on here. I know guys who need work," Galliwag said.

Ruth went out onto the porch and outside to where the football game was being played. Galliwag followed behind her. When David Paul passed the ball to Wen, Galliwag ran from behind and threw his weight at Wen, knocking him down onto the still-wet clay. His cheek scraped along the ground's surface. Ruth had seen the men play with the football, but she had never seen this type of aggression; the game just became serious and yet, by anything that could be said, it was just a rough sport; sometimes people were sacked, and men didn't whine, didn't howl about fairness or lack of fairness. Ruth eyed Galliwag for the move. Wen wiped the mud from his face, and Ruth noted some blood on his hand. He had a nosebleed. Galliwag's action worried her. She had tried to be honest with him with bad result. "Put the ball away and get on up to the orchard," Ruth said. She didn't know if she should call Wen into the house or let him go with the other men. "Wen, I need your help in the summer kitchen." Mix, Galliwag, and David Paul climbed into the cab of the truck and were soon off to pick apples. Ruth told Wen to clean off his face and meet her at her truck.

She took the loop that went around the pastures, the long way to the summer kitchen. She wanted to tell Wen so many things, and these thoughts circled through her mind. Ruth wanted to tell him that the hit he just took was far from friendly sport. She looked over at his scuffed dress shoes. "Galliwag hit you because I told him that you were a permanent hire and that you're an educated man." Wen was interested in her words. "Jobs are scarce since the lead mines closed, and you can expect jealousy. As for your education, I think it best that you hide that. Don't read your books at night in the men's house. Believe it or not, it is gossip. Hired hands, experienced farm workers aren't bookish. Men will not like you and can make life hard. The town can make life difficult for you if they find out that you're a writer whose books are banned."

Wen wrinkled his forehead. "There's more to the story, the books are about freedom."

"Take off those shoes and throw them out the truck window and hope Midget and Harry don't drag them back to the house as chew toys," Ruth said. "I'm going to be clear. Nobody here understands democracy. Free speech? Don't speak about it in Missouri. Ideas are nonsense to men with country know-how. You're in trouble because you're a smart man. The government has forbidden you to write." Wen looked surprised by the scope of her information. "I reread your mother's last letters to me, and I know all about causes, and the ideas that you articulate so beautifully. You should have never stopped being a poet. You should have stayed far away from politics." Wen turned his head away from her and stared out the side window. "I'm right," she said firmly.

"Do you know how the country has changed? This is the United States of America," Wen said without turning his face towards her. Ruth was silent. She was now aware of the truck's engine noise, the feel of her muscles pulling on the steering wheel. She turned her gaze away from the gravel road and tried to make eye contact with Wen.

"You're not a young man," Ruth said. She turned her attention back to the road. "But when you're my age, you'll see many things change, people die, the snowfall decreases, the mind doesn't respond as well as it used to, people move away, land is sold, whole forests are sent to the lumber yard, species become extinct, so why shouldn't a country change? You're resisting what seems inevitable, resisting the trek of planets around the sun."

Wen smiled and turned her way, then went back to staring out the truck's window. "I appreciate your thoughts," he said. "They make sense. But we're talking about what is fundamental. I've been forbidden to write, not because anything I write is revolutionary but because it is at the essence of our purported governmental values.

I'll be arrested if I scribble on a pad or express any sentiment." He paused. "Do you really want me to throw my shoes out the window?" Ruth nodded. Wen played with the heel.

Canning Apples

The truck stopped at the summer kitchen. Wen gave a seemingly last consideration to his shoes and decided to keep them for the day's work. Ruth led Wen to a locked door and opened it. She turned on the lights. Pots hung from the ceiling, and the large room was musty.

"The boxes in the corner contain canning jars. I need them washed; the soap is under the counter. You'll need to heat water on the stove so that wash water is hot, at least very warm." Ruth pulled the blinds to let in the natural light; windows were dusty with occasional cobwebs in their frames' angles. Wen lifted cardboard lids, and affirmed crowded jars. Ruth turned on the fan and opened the back door. "I think you'll work here for a couple of days. Probably make the hands jealous as all get out, but they need for the idea about your staying to set in." Ruth smiled and rubbed her hands together.

Wen filled caldrons with water and placed them on the stove. Hot water then went into a large sink. He removed the jars and swirled them in the soapy liquid. Wen was orderly, a characteristic that Ruth appreciated. She poured apples into a pressure cooker.

Ruth believed in physical labor, everyday she did as much work as her age allowed. She would often join the hands in the field and had grown to love the pungent odor of weeds and wild flowers. The farm represented the physical world to her. She looked at a scrape on Wen's face. She was reminded of what was tangible. There was, of course, something masculine about farm work. Ruth doubted that a younger woman would be allowed any authority with hired hands. The hands were occasionally bossy; she thought Galliwag was sending her a message by hitting Wen. He obviously thought her decision to hire an inexperienced man was wrong. Galliwag's move was dramatic; the hands' illustrative and dissatisfied moments seemed to manifest themselves with violence. Ruth was unsure about her change of heart. There was really no room for a greenhorn. Wen had little authentic interest in farming. She wondered how long it would take before he became bored with the work clothes and the fields. She imagined that, being barred from writing, his busy thoughts would emerge in oratory. She could only stand by her decision. There was a time when one needed to put away doubt and to trust one's own judgment. She would not let her thoughts vacillate any longer. "You don't want to give up those shoes, do you?"

Wen smiled, lifting a sugar sack and pouring its contents into a pot. "Doesn't matter. I don't want the only shoes that I have to become symbols. If they bother you, they can go. I'd rather not work barefoot. I'd not like to think that I'm giving up my identity or that it's stored in the toe like an old sock. I'm in Rome, so I can be like the Romans. I've been hired at a farm, and I'll do what you ask with as little resistance as possible. By everything you told me, the class issue burns strongly in the other men's minds." Wen was drying jars, was casual, calm. He picked up another jar from the rinse rack.

Ruth opened the lid of a pressure cooker, steam rose like a cloud. She took a fork and poked apples. "I imagine that half the strife in the world has been caused when people perceive difference. Galliwag does not think you're a wealthy man, but he knows that you're different. There's always a climate of anti-intellectualism in the country. I guess most suppose that big ideas are dealt with in church and the rest are out there for people to go along with." Ruth wiped her forehead with a cloth.

"Galliwag poses an irony for people like you. He is the kind that you advocate for, that you hope will benefit from your writing, and that man does not wish you well." Ruth waited for a reply. "He wouldn't understand two paragraphs of your writing, but would assume something wrong with it."

Wen moved a washed and dried rack of jars to Ruth's counter. "Galliwag would be in good company. I've been hit with an officer's stick for not turning over a manuscript. Galliwag's shove *is* the way people handle difference." Jars clinked and clattered as he moved another rack. "It is a time when dissenting views aren't tolerated." Wen shook his head. "This farm, this small town, isn't remarkable for its love of conformity. Do you need more sugar?" Wen asked. He brought her an unopened bag. "I'm just surprised by the extent of what people will conform to; we grew up believing that our country was an exemplum of liberty. I guess principles are just ideas and words. I don't see many forefather patriots rushing to defend my right to publish. I imagine that I'll be pushed to the ground a few times before the era changes." He stood close to Ruth as she blended cooked apples. "Oh, I never stopped being a poet. You said I stopped being a poet."

Ruth looked at him and acknowledged the idea of him being a poet. "I thought poets wrote about teal and orange sunsets and perfect roses." She measured three cups of sugar. "Those are your poet shoes, aren't they? Ah, nah, don't answer. Did you know that I had a son? He was not a poet. He was a Marine, and he was killed in Vietnam. He was 22, had just finished his degree at Washington University, had no use for the theoretical; he wanted to experience life, and a grenade ended it too soon. So you see I know that circumstances change. Oh, we can get comfortable, but life sends us challenges that knock us into that red clay without any conspiracy, events hit us much too hard so that we'd welcome a bloody nose or a broken bone. The universe turns upside down and we're left hanging onto what was saying turn it back, turn back time." Ruth looked down at the basket holding the uncooked apples. "I think that's it, the last of them." Ruth noticed that she had silenced Wen by revealing her lost son, and it satisfied her. They canned until late afternoon and cleaned up the neglected kitchen into evening. Ruth dropped Wen off at the men's house and was late to serve breakfast in the morning.

After breakfast, Ruth decided to stay behind. Canning tired her; she took a couple of aspirin for the arthritis in her shoulder. Today, she'd do strictly housework, would make herself scarce. Oddly, she had a great desire to lounge. She thought that the philosophical banter had drained her, or Wen's philosophical nature was rubbing off on her. It occurred to her that she might delight in the ethereal realm and play endless games with profound abstractions. She inwardly laughed at the possibility and became aware of the house's silence. She felt her socks slide across the hardwood floors and felt free from the hired hands and their daily dramas. In her mind, her responsibilities were fulfilled. She would give no orders today. It would be an experiment, to see if the men filled their hours from knowing a routine schedule. Ruth filled a bucket with water and planned to mop tile. The women's club once said she had the cleanest house in the whole county. She hoped that the men folk bragged on her fences and exhibitions at the fair. These were worldly things, and Ruth often wondered if one should invest so much pride in the approbations of others.

Harry and Midget were chained to the oak tree and were making a fuss, a commotion that usually meant a stranger was on the property. Ruth looked out through porch glass and saw the sheriff's car. She opened the door. The sheriff was approaching the house. "Mrs. Ruth," he said as a greeting.

"What can I help you with Clayborn?" The sheriff's hair was still blond despite his age. Ruth had gone to high school with one of his brothers. "Do you want the flatbed trucks for the summer parade?"

"It's Mike Galliwag, seems he owes back child support. I've papers to serve, his ex is taking him to court."

"Well, we can walk up to the men's house. But he doesn't stay here always, goes into town a lot." Ruth went back to shut the door and then began making her way up the hill, the officer followed her. She rang the doorbell at the house. No one answered after her third try. "I'm not sure where he is; he could be anywhere on the farm or not on the farm at all. I've not followed the men closely today." She laughed. "Sometimes I feel like they're children or visiting relatives; one just needs space. I don't know how much Galliwag owes for his oldest kids, but if somehow you could make that known to me, I will make good on it."

Clayborn smiled. "I noticed that there's a car with out of state plates in your lot. Do you have visiting relatives?"

"That would be Wendell Wilson's car. He is the son of my friend. She passed away last year," Ruth said.

"Wendell Wilson," Clayborn Burns said the name aloud. "I believe I've heard the name before. Is he a celebrity of sorts, maybe a writer? Maybe he's a political man. I've heard of Wendell Wilson."

"He's a farmhand. I've hired him as a permanent," Ruth said. "Can I get you a drink of something, tea or soda? The rain has quit, thank goodness. Now all we have is the heat to contend with. You let me know the extent of that debt, and I'll pay it. The men work hard on this farm. I know Galliwag isn't the best money manager and doesn't always set right priorities. Did you say if you wanted some tea?" Ruth walked the sheriff back to his car. Ruth's attention went to Mix's truck coming down the lane. "I think Galliwag is here." The truck stopped, and her hired hands were all in the vehicle. They opened the doors and walked over to Ruth and the sheriff. "Clayborn has some papers for you," she informed Galliwag. Mix shook hands with the sheriff. David Paul said nothing, changing directions and heading to the men's house. Wen sat on the porch steps, as if to rest. The sheriff handed Galliwag the summons.

But he was also interested in Wen, and eyed him from near the police car.

Ruth watched the sheriff finally walk over to Wen. "You're name is Wendell Wilson?"

"Yes sir."

"Why do I know your name? It's familiar to me. You've not been in some trouble with the law, have you, man? I'm going to run your name through our computers, and we'll see what's up with you." The sheriff walked back to his car and sat inside. Galliwag smiled at Wen. Mix went to stand by Ruth in case the sheriff's news might be shocking to her. But she went inside and poured herself some tea. She drank it quickly as if it would calm her nerves. Ruth had never thought to ask if Wen was in immediate trouble for a crime. She felt like she was waiting for a verdict about her own better judgment and good sense.

Wen came into the kitchen, followed by the sheriff. The sheriff thought it best if Wen revealed his situation, so the sheriff instructed the man of what to say. "Mrs. Ruth, I'm a nationally known agitator whose books have been cut off from distributors, in effect, they have been banned. I'm watched by law enforcement agencies because they want to make sure that I don't write and that my material is shut down before it reaches the public," he announced. "I thought you ought to know who you're really dealing with, so you can send him on his way," said Clayborn Burns. "I understand that he's waiting for a car part so he can go wherever agitators go. I can have those over to your place later today so he can get down the highway."

"Thank you for the information, Clayborn. You're kind to want to protect me, and the people of the county. Don't send anyone with car parts, we've ordered it and it's on its way. Wen isn't doing much agitating around here; he works eight to ten hour days with the herds. I've ordered some stone from the quarry and am going to have my men rebuild a wall along key boundaries of the farm. So they're busy men. Wen Wilson won't have time to write a letter. Cattle don't care about politics, never heard his name and are unmoved."

"You'd be wise to move him on," the sheriff said. "It's puzzling, Ruth, as to why you'd support such a character. Your husband served in the war, and I know you lost a boy in Vietnam." The sheriff scratched his head as a part of his point. "It makes me think that this Wendell Wilson has extra normal charisma and has taken you in. The people of this county would have a hard time believing that you're soft with an agitator," the sheriff said.

"I'll try not to speculate about what people think of me. He's a permanent hire, and I've felt called to help him, not to write books, but to put a roof over his head and to give him steady work with his hands. I've lived in this county off and on for close to 60 years. The community can judge me, but I hope they'll take into account everything. Wen Wilson has a job here." The sheriff smiled but there was not kindness in his eyes. Men like Wen were the huge bounty in ideological times. It would have been a prestigious notch for the law to have driven him out of town even though he had committed no crime. The word, "agitator" was rhetorically charged and was another name for the opposition's leadership.

"Agencies will be able to search your house as they please," the sheriff announced proudly.

"Warrants aren't necessary?" Ruth asked.

"They'll have sufficient cause as long as he stays here, and you pay his wages," the sheriff answered.

"Hardly sounds like America," Ruth said.

"Mrs. Ruth, that's the kind of talk that'll make the townspeople suspicious. Don't question how things are being done."

Mix entered the conversation. "Oh, Mrs. Ruth sees something about the man that reminds her of Danny. She's not a political woman beyond who wins the blue ribbon at the fair. I've seen her cut this man's hair, just the same way she used to cut Danny's. She's bought him shoes. She'll get her wits about her," the older hired hand told the sheriff. "Ruth Uppers has no use for shenanigans." Ruth was discouraged by Mix's attempt to help her. She had walked out on a limb for Wen, and she wasn't certain if she could explain why, but she had no intentions of backing down.

"I'd appreciate more you having more faith in the soundness of my mind," Ruth told Mix. "I cut his hair because his hair was long. I bought him shoes because he needed something to work in." The sheriff seemed bored by her explanations. Wen was embarrassed that the focus of the conversation was so much on him. "No, hear me good. Wen Wilson isn't a ghost; he is not my son, could not be my son with his independent nature. I'm not a senile woman whose grief has finally overwhelmed her."

The sheriff turned to her. "Think about it, Mrs. Ruth. At your age, the last thing you need is trouble." He gave Ruth a quick salute and was out the door. Ruth was left with the feeling that she had not said all she needed to say, and that she had said too much. Words grouped and regrouped in her mind. It was awful to feel passion and to not be able to express it. It was humiliating to have folks discount your mind. She looked at Wen and wondered about the fate of a silenced man. Expression had been his bread and butter. It was his means of making a living. He was now prevented from putting words on paper—this was perceived as a crime; this was the new establishment. The powers-that-be would make him a vagabond, a drifter with few ties to the community. The sheriff wanted him to make his way from town to town like a circus worker. She asked the men to return to their work and for Wen to stay behind.

She warmed water for tea on the stove. Wen appeared exhausted from the encounter with the sheriff. He held the end of a teaspoon with the tips of his fingers and made a dipping motion into the cup. It was as if he were anxious about the course of the next conversation. The sheriff's visit put reality in front of them. Ruth no longer needed to have Wen pass as a common hayseed. The facts were in the open, and the cards were on the table. But his identity was revealed still before people who would have no understanding of his ideas. The other hired hands only knew that he'd done "something wrong."

"I'm sorry," Wen said.

"Were you expecting it?" Ruth finally sat down.

"Not so soon." He stirred the tea in circles, seemed remarkably calm. "Eventually they find me, they track me." Wen paused. "I don't know whether you really want me to stay here. Now that they know where I am, they'll watch the farm, the trucks, they'll monitor your finances and your charitable contributions. You'll be watched because of me." Wen now searched her eyes for signs of fear and for pulling back.

"Where'll you go?"

"I don't know," Wen said. "I can speak at universities."

"You'll be arrested" Ruth told him. "If you stay here and mind your own business, work on the farm, I don't see how they can bother you. Oh they might come on the place, but that'll get old if they find nothing. They'll run you from town to town until there's nothing left of your talent and good sense. I don't think people are meant to live like gypsies." Wen took a large swallow of tea, put his elbows on the table and clasped his hands together. He rested his head on his folded hands and rocked back and forth. Ruth knew he was unsure of what to do. She thought about him being a silenced artist. "You can express yourself with your hands; look at the painters and sculptors. You can build a brick wall as high as a fortress. You can bundle hay and make designs in the pasture, maybe even chisel a stump. Your creativity doesn't need to come to an end; expression has many different modes."

"Why are you trying to help me?" Wen asked. "You said before that you'd do me no favors. But by allowing me to stay on here, you're putting yourself in jeopardy."

"Didn't you know that would be the case when you asked me for help?" Ruth paused. "It seems that you're a well-known man, a little notorious, and if I read like I used to, I'd have recognized your name as well. But to me and still to me you're Adda's son; she sent you to me. I don't mind telling you that it's been refreshing to have conversations with you."

"I don't think you understand the problem." Wen walked to the stove to pour more water for tea. "It's not something you can transfer to bricklaying or wood stacking. Thinkers are being silenced, oh not in well-publicized bans but in quiet erasure. Certain books just disappear like they never existed. Authors' names are wiped from databases. The news is purged," Wen said.

"I understood your struggle more when the sheriff was in my kitchen. If you're alienated you stand a better chance of losing. That's why I'm asking you to join my community, it might be rocky at first, because news will spread and men will talk, they'll call me senile and the whole nine yards. You'll be heckled the way polite people heckle with silence, whispers. But don't run any longer," Ruth entreated.

"I want to write," Wen said. Ruth stood and went to the refrigerator. She brought half of a roast to the table along with a cutting board and returned to the cupboard for bread and condiments. She began slicing the beef. Ruth went back to the refrigerator for cheese. Ruth apparently had sandwiches on her mind. "I want to write," Wen said louder, fearing that she didn't hear him the first time. She seemed to ignore him, was busy wrapping leftovers in plastic.

"Have a sandwich," Ruth said. "Often when I've a big decision to make, I eat. You eat something."

"Did you hear me?"

"When I was the librarian in St. Louis in the 1940s, I saw a protester beat bloody with a police officer's club. His group had slogans about peace and brotherhood. They hauled many of the demonstrators to jail, and it's bothered me for much of my life that I never inquired about the brutalized man. On anxious nights, I still can visualize his injuries. I'm certain that he didn't live, that somebody called his wife or parents and said he was the trouble."

"I only want to know that you heard me," said Wen.

"I'm trying to tell you that I heard you," Ruth replied. "Somehow I feel that you've already impressed the government, and if you go further, you'll not be safe and will be called the trouble." She finished making him a sandwich. "I'm not kidding you, I'm haunted by that assault; it has a dream-like quality to it as if its happening in the present and that one needs to wake up." She ate her sandwich in silence and watched Wen. At last she said, "Come with me." Ruth led him to the pocket doors and one door slid with difficulty across the hardwood floors. She took him into her library. The shelves seemed particularly majestic to Ruth since she was in the company of another bibliophile. Girlish joy overtook her senses, and she felt a fine pride, nothing haughty, and nothing superior, just an idea that she had preserved some of the finest books of the twentieth century. She saw Wen run his hands across the bindings, first vertically and then horizontally. Ruth took down a hefty volume and removed sheets of paper. She sat on the sofa, rereading her son's words:

"I'm optimistic today and have been for many weeks. Our troops are moving through enemy lines. I know that I couldn't feel such courage if I didn't believe that we're fighting for freedom.

"Mother, war is horrible, and people know it, so it must be for a just and honorable cause…"

She returned the pages without sharing them with Wen. "I knew that you loved books, that you had to love books, and you've almost denied it, but they're here on your farm, an entire library," Wen said.

"Everyone is allowed a past," Ruth chuckled. "You'd think I'd have them shelved to a system. I intended to but never got around to it. Don't be too excited; librarians aren't intellectuals in your sense of the word. They care about keeping the past for others. I suppose they care about well-documented research. They don't pretend to be scholars."

"Many of the big city libraries have been closed. It's said to be a drain of finances. You need a special permit to enter university libraries." Wen paused. "These books are truly wonderful. He held a volume to his lips and kissed it. "Could I stay for a little while and look through them?"

"I opened the doors especially for you; the quarry man is coming tomorrow and you'll need to be rested for heavy work. But you can come back after your daily work. You can come back all you want. This room isn't used much." Ruth showed Wen the dust on one shelf with her finger. "Maybe that will change. I suppose that I saved the books for a reason." She looked at the excited thinker, and his brown eyes sparkled with enthusiasm. "Go do you daily work," she said. He hesitated to leave the room. "You can come back after your farm work is done." Wen smiled, and Ruth sensed hope in his spirit, and she felt something similar in her own.

The morning rumbled with the sounds of quarry delivery trucks. The stone was stacked onto pallets and hydraulic lifts put them beside the broken Civil War wall. Ruth had thought about hiring professional masons, but Mix assured her that the hired hands could do the job. The men were arriving one by one. David Paul had the Dan-U Farms truck and once near the stone fence he began dumping mortar mix from its bed. Galliwag was walking down the road from the men's house, and Ruth stopped him. She wanted him to saddle the farm's only horse. In a couple of days, Ruth would have a birthday, and as a test of strength or as a badge of health, she would ride the farm's boundaries. It was important that she make the ride by herself, because she had much to contemplate, and a myriad of thoughts filled her mind. Once the saddle was on, Galliwag helped her onto the horse. She thought of splitting dry timber; her body was stiff, having lost some of its flexibility.

Galliwag hailed her on. She was gaining more confidence and was feeling comfortable with the animal's gait. Ruth rode to the broken wall, where she would start her daylong ride. Wen and David Paul were chipping out the loose and crooked stones. Ruth rode past them and up into the pasture. The cattle were interested in Lilly, probably thinking her the strangest and most unfortunate bovine for having a rider. Without moving at all, the cows intently stared at the horse and almost seemed to wonder about its business. The horse was a rarity; most trips across the pastures were done with motorized dirt bikes and ATVs.

She followed the broken wall up the grassy hill. When Danny was a boy, he scoured the ground beneath the wall looking for Civil War bullets. He'd write to local historians and detail his finds, and they would assure him that sections of the farmland had been places of battle. Ruth felt the pomp of history, an almost exaggerated feeling of importance about former events. The day was hot, and fluid trickled down her face. She could almost feel the heavy uniforms of yesterday's soldiers. Lilly approached the top of the hill. The high spot was a lookout. Men's thoughts were on their families and loved ones. They entertained ideas about their own mortality and about what would be left after their demise, perhaps children, a hand-built cabin. Posterity is considered the privilege of well-born and well-positioned men, but the poorer brother also hopes to leave a lasting mark on earth. Ruth thought of injury. She imagined a high-ranking officer wrapped in cords of golden decoration now viewing the end of a battle. She projected herself into the past, where men's limbs were blown off. Ruth heard their cries, though she could not answer them. The yellowish grass brushed against her boots. She could never answer them.

She rode Lilly down into the valley where cattle were watering at a center creek. She thought about following the shallow water stream and abandoning the wall. She could visualize men ducking low beneath its stone and concrete. When would the next shots be fired? Would they light up the sky like the orange of an evening sunset or would they put the grass in reaching flames? She felt a mock bravery; her nerve was steady along with her resolve. She had been put on this line as both a liberator and a protector. She had pulled the warrior's sword. She had danced her horse around the enemy. She had felt the burning wound.

Troops moved forward. The opposition retreated; they ran because they knew that their cause could not fortify them. The entire field showed men in motion, moving from the present danger. Horses stood on their hind legs in the confusion. Smoke hung in the air, above the weeds, lingering, much lower than the clouds. Eyes watered from spent gunpowder. She had conquered both the hill and the valley without a death. It was the conqueror's choice, to inflict destruction, and for all the scenes of war, for the brutality that was witnessed, the standoff was completed without actual carnage. Ruth felt satisfied with her victory, was pleased that Lilly seemed to know her way to the summer kitchen. She thought she'd regroup with a fresh fried egg sandwich and canned grape juice. The imagination worked up an appetite.

Mix called her on the walkie-talkie. "Ruth, we need you here. There's trouble with the quarry stone."

Ruth put Lilly on the dusty road, going past the summer kitchen, past the smoke house. Ruth thought it uncanny that horses seemed to know the way home. She suspected that they were in a great hurry to drop off their riders, and so had a mastered instinct for the barn. When Ruth finally arrived at the day's worksite, the quarry trucks were in place and had stopped their delivery. Two men wearing suits stood across from her hired hands in what looked like an argument's residual silence. She dismounted and walked over to Mix who was sitting on the ground. He pointed to the officious men and with his hand signaled that Ruth should deal with them.

As she approached one man, he prepared to show her his identification. He explained to her that he was a government agent and that the pallets needed to be inspected before the quarry could make the entire delivery. "You'll have to fill out papers. You'll have to explain why you've ordered so much stone," the man said. "We understand that you're reconstructing a wall."

"Historical preservation. The wall was built during the Civil War. It's my property and I'd like to maintain it." She looked at her idle workers. "Since when does government interfere with existing structures on private property? Are you men following the farm's business?"

"We want to inspect the pallets," one man said.

"Well, look at them so my men can go back to work," Ruth advised.

"It's more involved than that. We're going to remove each stone so that we can check between them," the official informed her.

"Then restack them when you're finished," Ruth said.

"We're under no obligation to do that. We've been assigned specific tasks and we're not putting them back on the pallets."

"You're taking them off the pallets," Ruth reminded them.

Legal Help

"No not exactly, he is taking the stone off the pallets." The official pointed to Wen. The other one can help." The man gestured for Galliwag to come forward. Ruth would say no more, but she mounted Lilly and rode her to the house. She was going to call her lawyer and ask him to refer her to a civil liberties expert; she'd be willing to drive into St. Louis for a conference. Her attorney, a tax specialist, agreed to come out to the farm and talk to the government men. After their discussion with Paul Davis, the officials agreed to leave and to present a search warrant in the event of another visit. Paul reminded the men that Ruth Uppers had an impeccable reputation in the county, and that many residents would be willing to sign affidavits on her behalf. Also, Dan-U Farms had a history of charitable giving.

Ruth wondered if anything her attorney had said really affected the government men's decision to leave. They acted without ignorance and knew Wen and probably knew her history as well. She thought about putting together a legal team to protect Dan-U Farms and its workers. The farm could not be managed with constant intrusions; it could not operate with daily or weekly delays in the work schedule. Ruth believed that today was a sample of things to come, random and absurd inspections. Wen would be singled out in front of the crew until it would be impossible from a credibility standpoint to keep him on. The town talk would rise and eventually people would suspect that there was some shadowy business in their midst. She wondered if her "impeccable" reputation could do battle with systematic harassment. She asked Paul Davis to arrange a conference about Wen Wilson.

Paul was surprised by what she was willing to do for the writer. "It'd save you money and a heap of trouble if you'd ask him to leave. Surely, he knows he's more than what he's worth. I don't know if the law can protect you when you've hired such a well-known agitator."

"They've closed many of the city libraries. Government permits are needed to use university libraries. Now, you tell me, that the law cannot protect my property from government inspectors or assure one man of the right to work as a hired hand. Paul, I know what Wen Wilson writes about, and it's no more than we learned about America as children. He repeats back to the masses what they used to understand about their world, like all men are created equal." Ruth paused.

"Don't sympathize with him in that way." Paul said.

"Why shouldn't somebody sympathize with trying to restore intellectual freedom in our country? Wen is not a criminal. He's a writer who is being made a scapegoat for broad anti-intellectualism."

"You're sounding like an agitator," Paul said.

"Will you put together and head up a legal defense team?" Ruth watched Paul look down at his lap. He was going to back down. He wanted no part of it. Ruth sensed his fearfulness.

"We all have families. I don't think my wife would let me become involved in this," he said.

"When I was a young librarian I witnessed a demonstration on the library steps. There I watched a protestor beat to death with an officer's club. He was demonstrating for peace. How vividly that scene comes back to me, like I could answer the cries or stop the pain. Age put events into proportion, and I am reminded of how I've turned away from my duties as a human being." Ruth stood to signal that their conversation was ending. She walked Paul to the outside door.

"You don't have a romantic attachment to this man, do you? He's moved you quite noticeably," Paul said.

"Come on, Paul. Don't color the story. Mix speculated quite publicly that Wen reminded me of Danny." Ruth didn't really think that Paul's question was worthy of an answer. "Give me the names of St. Louis attorneys if you get a chance, would you do that for me Paul? The weather's dried out, and I wouldn't mind driving into the city for a couple of days". Ruth extended her regards to Paul's family and said she hoped to see them at church. She was preoccupied while she chattered, watching Wen as he headed toward the men's house.

"Wen!" Ruth called. Wen came over to Paul's car and took off a cement encrusted glove to shake hands. "Paul, I'd like for you to meet Wendell Wilson whose mother was Adda. Now she grew up on what used to be called the Tymer place in Stone County. You see, Wen's roots are in the region. His mother was my friend during college." He shook Wen's extended hand, stood back, then examined him in totality.

"So you're Wen Wilson. You've caused a stir in this county. I can't help but think that you should not have come and that you should not stay."

Wen nodded his head. "Mr. Davis, have you been allowed to keep your law books?"

Paul put his hand on the car's door chrome handle; he was unsettled by Wen's question. "If you're like the majority of people in your profession you're issued a permit and are allowed to view law book sets at the court house in a room that is locked and unlocked. A record is kept of what you read."

"You're trouble, Wilson," Paul said. "You can't adapt to the new establishment. You question too much and are a smart man. But you're not smart enough to know when to keep your mouth shut; you're not smart enough to avoid dragging everyone down with you."

"Your practice is limited, right now you're staging representation, you don't know if you can actually advocate for anyone beyond real estate closings. When officials took the books from your office, you were stunned, but you vowed to be silent. What was their message and what else could they do to you, take your license, smear your name so that no court would hear you? Could they blackball you from practicing in your home state? Did you have the guts to ask others in the profession if their books were confiscated? Those government men this morning, I've seen them before, they follow me, they bully me, and then they go. They're not afraid of affidavits from good citizens. They'll be back without a search warrant. Don't doubt the ineffectiveness of a former profession," Wen said.

Paul seemed to escape; he threw his weight into the car and started its engine. "Ruth, I'll be in touch with you." Paul Davis backed down a long gravel driveway. In his hurry, he did not think to turn around in the circle. Ruth was surprised by Wen's passion and how he refused to be singled out this time. He wasn't going to let Paul have proud authority.

"Sorry," Wen said. He kicked at the ground with his boot. "You ought to go down and look at the wall. We're making progress." Ruth watched a car come up the drive. It was Connie Mae, Mix's daughter from his last marriage. Her pregnancy was near term, and she had some difficulty walking and was slow to get out of the car. She had grocery bags and packages. She often brought Mix canned soups and cereals. Connie Mae was close to Mix since her mother abandoned them both. Now, Mix worried about Connie. Mix regretted that she broke up with the child's father, and that she was seemingly on her own as far as finances. "I'll help you carry those bags, wait there, I'll be right with you," Wen told the wobbling woman. She loaded his arms, and they made their way to the men's house.

Ruth served breakfast early on her birthday, and the hired hands were out the door by 7:30. The turmoil of the last couple of days weighed on her. Wen's disclosure about the legal profession astonished her. Paul didn't dispute Wen's account of happenings, sealed law libraries. The two government officials were apparently assigned to watch Wen and his dealings. Ruth thought the men had an almost Hollywood quality about them, hired ruffians who were dressed in suits. They represented authority gone awry, like bullies in Sunday clothing. Today Ruth longed for peace, for no radical disclosures. She yearned for the simplicity in Galliwag's problems, gambling debts, DWIs, and angry women. She moseyed to the chicken yard. Ruth noticed that a brown hen was separated from the rest of the birds. The bird's isolation stood out today. The other birds might have rejected her. The hen might have enjoyed the large space surrounding her. She didn't need to follow in a line or cluck like the others. It was natural to feel sadness for creatures that were alone. Perhaps there was no need to pity her, for she had learned her comfortable position of the yard. Ruth carried a few fresh eggs to the house and saw Connie Mae's car was still in the lot. She stayed with Mix at the men's house, was probably doing her best to tidy the place. Ruth thought of the separated hen, and her compassion rose for the soon-to-be mother. Society would not be kind to Connie Mae or her child. The woman had no kind protector beyond a father who earned a small wage. Landlords would sternly assess her ability to pay rent. Doctors would question her about insurance and her ability to pay. The hospital would make her stay as short as possible. Connie could add another perspective to the true value of Wen's higher principles. The First Amendment and its preservation was a lofty goal when compared with Connie Mae's plight for survival. So Ruth was surprised to see them together. Wen carried a white insulated water jug and a folding chair. He set up the chair underneath the large oak tree across from the broken wall. Connie took her place in the chair while Wen chipped at the loose stones and then mixed concrete.

Mix came to the porch door and wanted to announce birthday plans. The hired hands planned a cookout, a steak fry at the men's house. Connie Mae iced the cake last night, and everyone was excited about a joint present; it was from all the men. Of course, Ruth was touched by her employees' gestures and could genuinely express delight. Mix saw that she was interested in Wen and Connie Mae, about their sudden friendship, the ease of their conversations.

"He's good to her, Ruth. Whatever else they say about him or whatever else he's done, he's respectful to women. He swept the floors when she said she was planning on it. He could treat her way different," Mix said. "David Paul says he was a teacher once because he underlines words in his books, like he was going to give a test. Hard to imagine him in trouble."

The two stood at the window watching the couple in the distance. "Connie Mae stirred a recipe, and he greased the pans. Isn't really like a man to be so helpful to a pregnant gal," Mix observed. "You've talked about his mother, how she was your friend, but you never say a word about his father."

"His father was a reader, another man too brainy for his own good." Ruth began to have flashbacks from that day on the library steps, and she resolved to stop the images. "Oh, I don't know what I mean by that. I didn't know his father well, Adda and I drifted apart. Marriage sometimes takes people funny places, away from the worn path. Wen's father was political. In those days, dissent frightened me, and I did my best to stay out of its way.

Mix looked confused. "*He* was the same as Wen, riled the government?" Mix shook his head. "Can't figure that man, never says bad words about anyone, people shove him, and he doesn't push back; he takes it." Mix was confounded. "That political nonsense doesn't start in the blood. He could've found his own life, settled down like any other man. Wen Wilson decided this," Mix said. Ruth nodded her head, indicating that she too thought he was a puzzle.

"If Connie Mae is going to stay at the farm until her time, it'd be best if she comes here." It isn't proper for her to be staying in a house with so many men. You can come to see her as you please, and Wen can visit, but see if you can't get her to bring her things over here," Ruth said.

"You're not going to miss your party?" Mix seemed to agree with the new arrangements.

"Not at all," said Ruth. She watched Mix leave. Wen and Connie Mae were now seated together underneath the towering and lone tree. The colossal tree grew outside the grove. It stood by itself with amazing grandeur. The limbs could bend and whistle in a roaring wind but no ears could hear their complaint. When the clouds turned violet, the oak stood regardless of harsh weather. Its solitary strength was mythic and an analogy for resolved wills. Perhaps Wen would mature into an oak, finding his deep roots in the county. Mix was right when he noted Wen's resilience, the way that he moved on after insults, even injury.

Galliwag was in charge of the grill and had spent part of the day in the men's kitchen making his special recipe for potatoes. Mix served drinks, knowing that Mrs. Ruth liked blended whiskey. He passed by Connie Mae, shaking his finger; there'd be no hard liquor for the expectant mother. David Paul was responsible for actually acquiring Ruth's gift, and his excitement was noticeable; he waited nervously like an actor about to go on stage. Galliwag muttered that Wen looked like the bridegroom, with his black pressed trousers and starched shirt. The hired hand had also bought a new pair of two-tone shoes, and Galliwag could hardly contain himself. "You shouldn't have dressed so pretty for us."

"Gosh, Wen, did ya use a bar of soap? You're the cleanest stone mason in the whole state," David Paul said jokingly. "Your face even shines; they're gonna put that glowing face on a quarter."

Ruth sipped whiskey and also wondered about Wen's clothing. She said nothing and tried to enjoy the festivities. Mix brought out his guitar and sang slow country songs.

Galliwag sang along in an exaggerated way, about broken hearts, and missed alimony payments. Galliwag was a performer, flipping steaks with gusto, downing full beers in two swallows. "Play something we can dance to," Galliwag swayed his hips while he watched the grill. "Play a song about Dan-U Farms' very own outlaw." Galliwag made up a song. "Wen Wilson, Wen Wilson, prettiest rebel man the women ever seen, Wen Wilson, Wen Wilson, Ahoo, Ahoo." Wen smiled at Galliwag, knowing that the man was spitefully mocking him. Wen went inside with Connie Mae and helped her set the table.

"He's not going to take that forever. You're pushing your luck, Mike Galliwag," Ruth said.

"Think he'll read to me, Mrs. Ruth?" Galliwag adjusted the air going to the grill. "He's rebuilding that wall, takes Mix's little girl down to the site, and he shows off his muscles. I've heard him talk when he thinks we're not paying any attention. And you know what, Mrs. Ruth, he thinks he's the brightest boy in town. But I think he's stupid and a fraud."

"Did the money help with your back child support," Ruth said.

"Yeah, thank you, Mrs. Ruth." Galliwag became quiet, appeared to be in thought. " I'd better go see if they're ready in the house. Happy birthday, Mrs. Ruth, you're swell to your people." He winked at her, set down his barbeque fork, and went into the kitchen.

Ruth followed Galliwag into the house. Connie Mae was seated in an upholstered chair; she was in pain. Wen and Mix knelt beside her. Galliwag removed a large platter from the cabinet and went out to bring in the steaks. A pink birthday cake was situated in the middle of the table.

Wen stroked her hand; a kind expression was on his face. "I might be the only one sober enough to drive her into the university hospital in St. Louis. It'd be terrible to be pulled over for speeding with a couple of drinks on the breath." Wen checked the time, trying to estimate the trip.

David Paul rushed forward and presented Ruth with a receipt. "Happy birthday, Mrs. Ruth. We chipped in and paid the registration fee for 'Earthquake' in the blue ribbon bull contest at the fair." He smiled, having done his part before Connie Mae's condition became the only interest. David Paul returned to a stool in the corner of the living room. Galliwag stood by a plate of warm steaks.

"Thank you," Ruth acknowledged each of her hired hands.

"Maybe she don't want you to drive her to St. Louis," Galliwag said. "Maybe she wants her dad to take her. They might haul you away dry as a drought. You're not designated by anyone," Galliwag sneered. Mix was concerned. Wen remained close to Connie Mae.

"Wouldn't be a bad drive," David Paul said.

Wen asked Ruth for the keys to the SUV. "I'm comfortable driving her in. If you want to come, I'm fine with that. The interstate shouldn't be busy this time of night. A friend's baby isn't born on your birthday too often." Wen began to help Connie up, to help her find her things for an overnight stay, and began gathering shampoo, lotion, and toothpaste from the bathroom. "Do you have a robe?" Connie Mae shook her head, so Wen took his and packed it into a suitcase. "Now the important thing is not to worry, babies are born daily, and yours is going to be fine. You concentrate on thinking of a name. Names are really very important," Wen said. Mix put her slippers into the bag. He smiled at Wen and was grateful for his reassurances. Wen, Mix, and Ruth would drive Connie to the city hospital. When the group left the men's house, Galliwag flung an empty plate across the counter and it dropped and shattered in front of Wen. Wen kicked the broken glass aside from impatience more than anger. Galliwag was pleased with the reaction. Ruth wished that Wen had not responded at all, Galliwag was only waiting for the right moment.

Ruth unlocked her door and went into her house. The message light was blinking on her telephone answering machine. She pushed the button, intending to listen to the message as she packed an overnight bag. Paul Davis left names and numbers of attorneys in the St. Louis area. She scribbled them onto a phone pad, ripped off the tiny sheet, and put it in her purse. Ruth took the keys to the Suburban down from a hook and made her way to the porch and the other travelers. "I think this might be my most eventful birthday," Ruth said.

Ruth elected to drive because Galliwag had a point about Wen speeding into the city. He needed no alcoholic beverages to arouse the law's interest. Mix sat in the passenger seat. Wen and Connie Mae were in the back. Ruth observed Wen's tenderness as he attempted to calm Connie. He leaned her head against his chest. "I bet you weren't expecting this tonight, made Mrs. Ruth a cake and bingo, you're off to the hospital. If it's a boy, you're going to name him Patrick Henry or Henry Clay, aren't you?"

Connie laughed. "What if it's a girl? It's going to be a girl. I put pink icing on the cake."

"Ah, but the sky was blue today. I've never seen a bluer sky," Wen said.

"Is there any particular meaning to cloudy days? Is that when you have a colicky baby?" Ruth joined in.

"Not going to name my grandson Patrick Henry, sounds too much like an Irishman." Mix added. "Blue skies, cloudy skies, you only need to watch it if it thunders. Then you're gonna have a bossy little girl and when she grows up she runs everything with an iron frying pan."

"Daddy," Connie was delighted with her father's whimsical speculation. She enjoyed the light conversation to the point that she had almost forgotten her pain. "I'm going to name him Richard Dale Mix II."

"Sounds good," Ruth said.

Mix hooted. "Don't want to do that, a little highfalutin' to my taste. They'll be chasing him around like Wen Wilson." A sudden silence interrupted the fun. "What did you ever do, man? Why you'd think you robbed a bank or bopped an old lady over the head?" Mix said.

"Did neither," Wen said.

"Little advice, Wen. You'd better watch Mike Galliwag. In town, he runs with rough fellows. I've never seen him so focused on anyone as you. He seriously dislikes you," Ruth said.

"I'm in the company of people who do like me," Wen said. "I try not to worry about the others." A semi-trailer whistled past. "I remember thinking as a kid that writing was the noblest profession. The writer informed, he entertained, and he offered flaws and gifts to other people. It seemed like a job that couldn't go wrong. One could find a wife and get a house in the country." Wen paused. "I couldn't have known the nation's course or the unpredictable times."

"You know what's going to happen at Dan-U Farms; that broken wall will be in need of repair when we get back; there will still be four herds of cattle, the pastures will be cut into hay," Ruth said. "Paul Davis called with names of attorneys in St. Louis. We can make an appointment while we're there and go in and see somebody that might be able to help us."

"Mrs. Ruth, you're the kindest woman I've ever known, fair with employees, a contributor to the church. So pardon me when I tell you how widespread this is. City attorneys are no different and will act no differently than Paul Davis. Books are stored at the county seats. The idea is to keep men ignorant and compliant with whatever comes their way. An appointment with a big city firm will only be another tracking point for them."

"Ya okay Connie Mae?" Mix turned back to his daughter.

"She's going to be fine," Wen said. He stroked her hair and momentarily seemed to forget his circumstance.

Mix thought this was an appropriate time to admonish Wen. "Mrs. Ruth says that your dad was a political man. I say drop it. All it's given you so far is a heap a trouble and it don't seem to be letting up. You're a good man. It's time to be your own man and stop living your father's life." Ruth was stunned that Mix had revealed his knowledge about Wen's father.

"Someday I'll tell you about my father," Wen said. "I think this is your exit," Wen told Ruth. Ruth followed the exit and found the hospital. She dropped her passengers off at the emergency unit and went to the elevated parking ramps. Ruth was discouraged with Wen's assessment of the legal system. If the system was a broad sham, what was her recourse for protection? Rights were merely words and could be enforced or ignored arbitrarily. She parked the Suburban and reached into her purse, looking for a small paper with the attorneys' names and numbers. She crumbled it in her hand, so that she would not be tempted to make any appointments.

Ruth became acutely aware of her aloneness. There were rows and rows of empty cars but not a person in sight. Some change dropped from her billfold and it sounded on the stained concrete. She walked down what appeared to be a road to the elevator. She entered the elevator and was once again entirely alone. A sign read, "Please use stairs in the event of fire." Her mind trailed into the past, and Ruth was standing in the midst of the demonstration, the same scene, and the police officer was cuffing protesters. She tried to stop the memory; she affirmed to pull herself together as one might halt tears. She shut her eyes trying to block visual prompts.

Tonight, she could not relive Wen Wilson's father's demise. What would Wen tell Mix about his dead father? What did he know? How many times she wanted to say, "I was there. I saw it." She wanted to expiate her guilt for being a sheep-ish onlooker on account of her youth. The world wasn't political to a girl raised in Alcott County and who had gone to college on the money from selling fresh produce. She never called the hospital that night because she was afraid. She had never seen the consequences of clashing viewpoints. Words were simple in the country and had simple values. Peace was generally considered to be good. Ardent young men were not beaten because they camped out on the library steps and said they wanted peace.

A yellowish light beamed into the natal care waiting room. Connie Mae had been taken to a birthing room. The waiting room chairs were blue paisley in a vinyl fabric. They had stainless steel armrests. Mix fidgeted, leaned on one hip, and then the other. Wen read magazines and regularly checked his watch. He seemed like a man in a hurry, that others would have to pick up the pace, because he had engagements to keep. A tie was strung loosely around his shoulders, giving the appearance that the actual knotted item was for another meeting. After an hour, an Asian-American doctor came through the double doors. "The father?" he said.

Mix stood up, and the doctor gently pushed him back into the chair with a chuckle. "The baby's father," he said. The doctor took Wen by the hand and led him into another room. "You're shy. No time to be shy," the doctor said. Mix and Ruth exchanged glances, were amused by the mistake. Soon Wen came out in a surgical gown, announcing the birth of a boy.

"He looks more like his mother," Wen winked about the misunderstanding. "Connie Mae is fine," he said. Ruth was relieved, but now her thoughts went to the farm. She wasn't sure about having Galliwag and David Paul alone for very long. Both men worked best under supervision.

Mix shook Wen's hand in a hearty manner, as if Wen was responsible for the healthy child. "I worried about her the whole time, sometimes I worried she'd spend all her money on me and not eat right. Wen, she'd bring me groceries two or three times a week.

Wen checked his watch and began to knot his tie. Ruth was concerned about his meeting in the city. But she wasn't his mother and had no business prying into his affairs.

"Are you going to be safe," Ruth said.

"After what I just witnessed, I feel blessedly immortal." He smiled fully and was uplifted in his heart.

"You're not immortal, so come back to the motel with us. Are you speaking tonight?" Ruth held her breath.

"I need money. I need money," he whispered to her. "I think I'm getting married soon," Wen said, so Mix couldn't hear.

"You're coming with us, no more excitement for a while." Wen checked his watch again. "No please, Connie Mae needs a live stone mason and not a stone cold activist. Wen, we can talk about money and ways to increase your earnings. At any rate, we need to talk about you joining a lecture circuit. I know I've no right, but I'm begging you to cancel the rally."

"Your own man," Mix said, slapping Wen on the shoulder. "Be your own man," he told him.

"There'll be several speakers. I'll be missed but am under no contract." He went to use the phone and came back shortly. "Ruth, sometimes I think you don't understand what I'm trying to accomplish, what I want to bring back to our country. You told me not to run, and I'm working on doing that. I'm unsafe when current events are secret. I'm not safe when they can erase my name and take my profession," Wen declared. "I'm not safe when I have to walk around in disguises and change my language. Then I've been totally robbed."

A nurse entered the waiting room. "Connie Mae is ready for visitors." Wen unknotted his tie and gave it to Ruth. It was a sign of at least temporary surrender. She carried it into Connie Mae's room and later tucked it into her purse. Ruth knew now that she would not make him quit his political activities. He had planned on driving into St. Louis before Connie's pains. Farm work had fueled his desire for a public life and a private one. Ruth didn't doubt his sincerity when he spoke of marriage. Wen was transforming into his own man.

"His name is Hugh Richard Mix," Connie Mae announced to the group. In the morning, the nursing staff hurried with discharge paperwork; they were aware of her insurance's limited responsibility. Ruth wanted to make two stops, one at the courthouse and another at the Presbyterian Church. She went over her plans with Wen and Connie Mae to see if there was any objection. She had Wen's tie in her purse, and they could stop at a mall on the way out of town. Mix was ambivalent about the proposed marriage. He liked Wen but, however likable, Wen Wilson was a man with a price on his head, maybe not today, but sooner or later, the government would win. A solitary man had little chance against the system. Ruth knew Mix worried about Connie Mae's and the baby's future. Connie Mae would be involved in Wen's politics. It was like having your daughter marry Jesse James.

Ruth called her minister and asked for a special favor. She wanted a brief wedding after the Sunday worship service, a simple exchange of vows. The minister questioned Ruth as to why the couple did not want more of a private ceremony. Ruth explained that two lives were being changed, and the act of commitment called for many witnesses. Ruth purchased a wedding dress for Connie while the crew waited in the Suburban. Ruth also bought Wen a fresh shirt and trousers. Ruth and Mix would stand up for the bride and groom.

On Sunday, in Alcott County, at the tail end of the 9:30 service, Wendell Wilson married Connie Mae Mix in front of a packed Presbyterian congregation. Ruth held Hugh at the altar. The townspeople had heard rumors of Ruth Upper's slow descent into the lower classes, and the wedding only affirmed their confusion. Ruth had donated every one of the church's stained glass windows, and when her husband was alive, she ran Meals on Wheels.

She was a reliable contributor for special projects. Most people were aware that her dead son was a decorated war hero. Ruth Uppers also operated the largest cattle farm in Alcott County. Now she was standing at the altar and witnessing the marriage between a hired hand's daughter and an outlaw. Women in bright hats, teal, magenta, and azure, assessed the bridegroom. His name traveled down every pew and returned, like the offering plate.

The women were surprised that he didn't appear thuggish or vulgar, and they tried their hardest to remember just what he had done. He was some sort of criminal, an element of riffraff.

Ruth was getting up in years. Was it possible that her mind was going and that she was no longer a good judge of character? Everyone knew she was proud of community ties and contacts. She had received awards for citizenship and volunteer service. Paul Davis had suggested that Ruth had a romantic attachment to the handsome visitor. His theory was no longer plausible. Then there was the child. Everyone knew that the baby wasn't Wen Wilson's. It seemed like outsiders were adopting each other with Mrs. Ruth's blessing. In fact,

astonishing to onlookers, Ruth seemed genuinely
fond of her company.

After the service, Ruth hugged friends of
many years, and was bursting with joy about
what had just transpired. She introduced Wen and
Connie Mae as if they were from registered gentil-
ity. She brushed a speck of lint from Wen's coat to
enhance his appearance. He looked sharp. Elderly
ladies surrounded Hugh, actually formed a group
around the baby. Ruth noted that the bride was
tired from the unexpected excitement, and Ruth
resolved to hurry her home. Wen had asked if
he could turn the summer kitchen into a house,
move the junk out from the back storage. Ruth
considered his idea as a possibility but, for now,
she was moving the newlyweds into her place;
they could occupy the rooms on the other side of
her kitchen, which included close access to the
library. Other arrangements might be made later.

A Family Now

David Paul cooked sausages while Ruth took orders on eggs. She put scrambled eggs on her menu many years ago, and sometimes regretted the extra effort in making them. Galliwag poured coffee and was the first to be seated at the breakfast table. Galliwag looked at the bags in the adjoining living room. He recognized Wen's suitcase; he swallowed a mouthful from his cup. Mix entered the room and was unusually cheerful. "Connie Mae had a boy," he told Galliwag.

"I heard," Galliwag said. "I also heard you let Wen Wilson marry your girl." Ruth put a platter of biscuits on the table.

"She's not a girl and can marry as she pleases," Mix replied. Ruth could hear Hugh cry, and she supposed that was the reason that Wen was late for breakfast. Finally, Wen came to the table. Galliwag noted Wen's new residence, and the freedom he had been given in the boss' house. The new husband was dressed in concrete-spattered work clothes and carried his canvas gloves. He yawned throughout breakfast and was quiet. Hugh was up a good portion of the night. Ruth also suspected that Wen was coming to a realization of his private life; he was no longer alone and was no longer a free spirit. He honored words and had taken a vow. Ruth hoped that personal and practical concerns were on his mind.

She hoped that he entertained ideas about making a wife happy and that he would take a hiatus from politics.

Galliwag ate his breakfast, cutting down hard on the food with his fork. Ruth doubted that his silence was on account of a truce but rather, because Wen had seemingly acquired new status on the farm. The surly hired hand now knew that Wen was a favorite with the old woman. He had suckered her, impressed the retired librarian with his books and crisp white shirts. Wen was on Mix's good side; he married the man's abandoned daughter and planned to raise her son. David Paul was neutral about Wen. Indeed Galliwag was outnumbered with his criticism, yet his anger was pushed to a deeper level. Galliwag was jealous of Wen.

David Paul stood and took his dirty plate to the sink. He put on his ball cap and headed toward the porch door. Ruth could hear the young hired hand talking to Clayborn Burns. She wondered what was next. Galliwag sneered at Wen, thinking that the sheriff was here for the privileged one. Ruth hurried Mix and Galliwag off, and they hesitated to go. She said she wanted privacy.

Clayborn threw a newspaper down on the kitchen table in front of Wen. "You've been in St. Louis, haven't you ,man?"

"Yes," Wen said.

"Somebody tipped you off about that rally at the university. Isn't that right? Well, the man that spoke at your appointed time was shot, and agitators are calling it an intended hit against Wen Wilson. You see, the bullet came from outside the stadium, from a gun with a high-powered scope. We're pleased as punch that you're alive, but why did you cancel? Who tipped you off? We can sit here all day until you talk. Who told you to go home?"

"I guess it was my guardian angel," Wen said. "I stayed with Connie Mae Mix at St. Joseph's Hospital while she had her baby. I married her at the Presbyterian Church on Sunday morning. Ruth Uppers and Richard Mix were with me the entire time. Now I have a wall to rebuild, and there's not a lot more for me to tell you." He stood, and the sheriff let him pass.

"We're watching you, Wen Wilson," the sheriff said in a loud voice. Wen shut the porch door and gathered his tools. He began walking to the worksite, going by the sheriff's car.

"One of these days, that bullet won't be mistaken and an innocent man won't be a target."

"He can't hear you," Ruth said. "He's down the lane." Ruth watched Wen unpack stone from a pallet.

"Ruth, I'm telling you this because you need to know. Wen has been banned for writing, but he's sold a manuscript to a Canadian distributor and when copies of that book reach the United States, your bricklayer is in deep trouble. American authorities aren't going to let him write lies and get away with it. How that puny man out there became a national item is so beyond me," Clayborn said. "Goodwill is not coming your way for having him here. I think most people think that you've gone daffy from age or you've confused him with the lost son."

"I've done neither," Ruth said. "Clayborn, Wen would have been better off without the news you brought today. He's not a suspect in any crime, and you came to harass him and scare him. Please, don't do that again. As for his writing, I'm not aware of any contracts or manuscripts. He doesn't write on this farm. He also has a family, and you need to leave them alone. I don't like talk about mistaken bullets and targets. What has the world come to?"

Connie Mae entered the kitchen with her infant. She was surprised when both Ruth and the sheriff stopped talking; they hesitated to exchange words because of the new bride. In town, it was widely believed that Wen Wilson might have either rescued Mix's daughter or that he saw some perverse advantage in marrying into a lower class. Maybe it was a part of a political theory, and the move had a theatrical quality just the same as a writer putting down stone. Galliwag suspected a heady design, as regular men do not take on other men's paternity responsibilities. Wen confused people, the well-dressed academic figure or the splattered stone mason? People didn't understand the accusations against him, why Wen couldn't write.

"Mrs. Wilson," the sheriff tipped his hat. He picked up his copy of the St. Louis paper, and was on his way.

"I didn't like the sound of that," Connie Mae told Ruth. "He was threatening Wen," she said. Ruth appreciated Connie Mae's naiveté, her preoccupation with the events in her own life. Ruth imagined Wen explaining inalienable premises of law to her. Ruth believed that Connie Mae would remain in the dark about much of Wen's work. She was not sufficiently educated to appreciate her husband's theoretical essays. Ruth believed he wanted it that way. In his private life, he did not want to discuss or analyze ideas, he only wanted company. After a few days of rest, Connie Mae returned to her chair beside Wen at the wall. Hugh slept in a carrier, as summer waned into fall, stone by stone, a Civil War wall was rebuilt.

Autumn brought peace on Dan-U Farms. Mix, after some consideration, was elated with his daughter's marriage and, if possible, he took more interest in the cattle operation. Mix sensed that Connie Mae and Wen's union elevated his own position on the farm. Mix felt more responsible, was perfectly dependable. Galliwag wasn't so intent on acting up since Wen was a family man. Mike Galliwag's own weakness was too little commitment to his children. He liked the taverns and pool halls. Galliwag liked to gamble on the boats in St. Louis. If Wen wanted to buy baby food with his extra wages, Galliwag had no comment.

David Paul recognized diversity about the farm these days. Connie Mae had taken over cooking breakfast: the farm was no longer about men. In the mornings, Hugh joined them at the table in a highchair. By November, it was obvious that Wen and Connie Mae were expecting a second child. Ruth was delighted; and she suggested that an addition be built for the main house.

Ruth reveled in the feeling of community. Farms were meant to "grow" people of all ages, from the very young to the old. Connie Mae bought Wen a sweater for his birthday, and he wore it daily. After fieldwork, after driving the hay truck, and, after a shower, he often retired into the library. Ruth knew that he was acquainted with every title and knew what each book had to offer. Baby Hugh stacked volumes on the floor while Wen read with zeal; the father wanted to expose the child to bound knowledge. The child's toys were scattered about the room. Ruth sat in a covered chair, liking both the toddler's prattle and Wen's firm silence.

"What do you suppose happened to the agents?" Ruth asked.

Wen looked up from his paperback. "I don't know. There're around. I don't think it would be too informative to track a cowhand," Wen laughed. "He moved a herd to the East pasture today," Wen mimicked their possible notes. "They'll be back when the Canadians come through and finally distribute my work. We can appreciate the lull in their actions, but they've not gone away. There're signs that things are getting worse, there're detentions without charges. More lawyers are being locked out of the system; young people are handpicked for law school and are required to take party loyalty oaths," Wen said. He picked up Hugh and rested the child on his hip. He walked around the room. He stood facing a wall of books, with his back to Ruth. "I'm thinking about joining a lecture circuit."

Ruth felt adrenaline course through her body. "If you do, you'll not be safe. Clayborn Burns brought you a newspaper article about a man who was mistakenly shot in your place. Is that true? After you left, he warned that Canadian distribution of your book would break the law, and that there were men who would not hesitate to kill you. Does Connie Mae know about your speaking plans?" Wen turned and faced Ruth, then shook his head. He put the child down.

"You're not going to change the country, and I won't accept your selfishness," Ruth said. "Perhaps the country will change with time, and you can return to your literary profession. But understand Wen, these determined men are talking about your life, and you won't be able to express much after that's gone. Men like Galliwag will shovel your writings into a hole in the ground or make a bonfire with your precious words. Please assume rougher characters, some men who do not value freedom."

"People do value freedom," Wen insisted. "It's innate."

"People don't know what you know; you're not the right man to convince them that the country has undergone a radical change, because you see, you're seen as the radical. It might be a clever ploy on their part. Officials have painted the wrong picture of you, and they have made it stick; they've defined you. Most people don't feel that their rights are being taken away. Men like Paul Davis will have to come forward and tell their stories." Ruth sighed. "Cancel the Canadian distribution of your book and your speaking plans," Ruth said without apology.

"Come to the St. Louis Library with me, and then you can say who is radical and tell me about what people do and do not know," Wen said with passion. "I'm serious. I want to take you there."

Connie Mae entered the library in a quilted robe; she had already gone to bed. And yet she seemed to exaggerate her tiredness, yawning, rubbing her eyes. She gathered Hugh's stacking books and began to return them to shelves. "He makes a mess in here, doesn't he?"

"He's okay," Wen told his wife. "Take him to bed. I'm coming in a few minutes."

Ruth watched Connie Mae shrug her shoulders. Connie Mae knew that her husband was involved in a conversation that he did not want to leave immediately. It was as if she competed with the library for her husband's attention. On occasion, Connie would join him, and he read her his favorite poetry, but frankly, Ruth suspected that it bored the new wife. Whatever the case, she never stayed long in his adopted room and often called him to bed.

"Ruth is going to ride into St. Louis with us tomorrow. Your doctor's appointment is at11:30. I'd like to take her by the city library and show her some things." Connie Mae was disappointed with Wen's news. She had looked forward to the ride into the city and to having her husband to herself.

Ruth wore traditional dress clothing for her visit to the city's library; her suit was a wool blend and an earth tone. She wore flat black shoes with silver buckles. Her gray hair was neatly combed around her head and fluffed at the forehead. Whatever she saw in the city, she would appear dignified. Connie Mae was dropped off at her obstetrician's office, and Wen began his way, zigzagging through mid morning traffic, to the library. Buses puffed out black smoke. Taxis maneuvered at great speeds and then came to sudden stops. Steel workers exited a factory and were off for lunch. They failed to remove their hardhats, as if the protective helmets were attached to their heads. Down another block, well-dressed men carried briefcases and morning newspapers. Wen looked for a place to park along a metered street.

Once out of the vehicle, Wen put his arm through Ruth's and escorted her in the most mannerly way. He cleared the path through loitering crowds, through people conversing in groups. "Excuse us," he aggressively cut through mixing businessmen and standing deliverymen. Finally, the sidewalk was abandoned, and Ruth began to recognize the part of town. Wen and Ruth came to a public building. Squirrels jumped out of the trash cans that were situated near ornate benches. Horse drawn carriages rode in front of the white stone building.

"It's been turned into a tourist attraction," Ruth said.

"Hmmm…See any tourists around?" Wen replied. He walked her up the steps until they came to two heavy doors. "I've a friend who's a superb locksmith, and we can thank him for this." Wen turned the lock and gently opened the door. He let Ruth in and followed behind her. "Familiar, Mrs. Ruth?" The pair walked through a disheveled lobby. Books were piled on a return counter; some had fallen on the dusty floor. Books were knocked off shelves, and spray paint messages marked the walls. Chairs were stacked up along the walls. "The elevator doesn't work, so we'll have to use the stairs," Wen said. Tables were turned on ends on the second floor. Entire shelves were tipped over, and fallen books made it difficult to walk. "Now Ruth, tell me about why I need to shut my mouth; this makes me want to yell." He began to raise his voice. "It makes me want to write so everybody will know." His voice echoed on account of the building's high ceilings. "It makes want to say, 'this is wrong.'"

A trapped bird flew against a skylight, and the noise scared Ruth. What could prompt such disgust for knowledge, and when books were a target, where did reason come in? Suddenly, she felt overdressed as if she had expected her old colleagues to greet her at the door and a reunion would follow. With this sight, her past was gone; Ruth expected that a part of civilization was passing on as well. Ruth imagined the human arms that toppled entire library sections. What bitter sentiment directed them or was there only mind-lessness to the action? Ruth tugged at Wen's sleeve, signaling that she was ready to go.

Ruth went into the obstetrician's waiting room with Wen. Connie Mae had been waiting with Hugh for over a half hour, and she wasn't pleased with either of her rescuers. "Next time, the doctor wants you to keep Hugh," she scolded her husband. Then her voice was light, "Honey, I'm expecting twins. The doctor hears two heart-beats, says I'm getting big too soon." Wen smiled sheepishly as if fate had dealt him a strange hand to go along with his other passions.

"Twins, two?" he said. Ruth held Hugh and offered her congratulations. "Don't tease me now, Connie Mae," Wen said. The wife wasn't joking, and she was proud and happy. She only hated waiting so long to share her news. Wen drove back to Dan-U Farms without a word.

Ruth was broadly anxious when she arrived home. Her community was going to grow, and the main house was not going to be large enough to suit Wen's and Connie Mae's family. In her mind, she reviewed the names of local architects and contractors with the thought of building an even more private addition, another bedroom, two baths, and a nursery. She worried about the stress of the unexpectedly large family upon the couple, and was reminded to pay her hired hands' health insurance premiums. Ruth prayed that the twins would be as healthy as Hugh, and that they would be a blessing to Wen in his domestic life. Then a sense of gloom overcame her, and she was reminded of scenes in the city library. Wen was challenged by the suppression of knowledge and by the utter ugliness of violent anti-intellectualism. The movement had gone beyond silencing men and women of ideas; it had cut into the core of culture, defiled language, and the keepers of history.

A thousand images of Galliwag came to mind, the way he rode his motorized dirt bike so close to the cattle, the way he slammed the tailgate on the farm pickup, the way he threw tools at a worksite. His physicality was overdone, was more than what was necessary to achieve an end. She remembered Galliwag hurling his body at Wen, knocking him down into the mud. During work on the Civil War wall, Galliwag lobbed stones at Wen, and he was to catch them. Angry arms also tore at the city's library shelves and sought to render the collected information useless, irretrievable, a hodgepodge of paper objects. Ruth commiserated with Wen's passion about the helter-skelter relics in a public building. She recalled the sound of the lone bird hitting the skylight, and she wondered if there was a viable and safe exit for a muted writer. Ruth still concluded that only a home could provide refuge for Wen, and he needed to immerse himself in the community, no matter what the reception. Sharleen Davis, Paul's wife, had told the church circle members that Wen was a spy from Zambeenia, not Zambia, but actually Zambeenia. Ruth wasn't much of a geography scholar, but she doubted that such a state existed. Sharleen reported that Wen arrived at Ruth's door like a vacuum cleaner salesman; put his foot in the door through fast talking, and he was now a permanent member of the household, along with the old hired hand's daughter and her toddler. Ruth mused that spies from Zambeenia were particularly clever, maybe even brilliant. These spies were perhaps the only ones who could look at a faltering democracy without resorting to fairy tales and late twentieth century movie plots. Ruth imagined Wen's economy car, and for the sake of drama, she added wing-like doors and ejector seats. The car could reach record speeds on both land and water.

Then she imagined Wen as the fast-talking vacuum cleaner salesman. He was perhaps the only one to approach the side porch without feeling the bites of Harry and Midget. The salesman talked the collies into submission also. Wen cleaned the carpeting so thoroughly that Ruth could not fathom her next 20 years without the salesman and his miracle shampoo. He had dazzled her, and the rest was history. He impressed everyone he met with the soap solution, and so a bride soon came his way. The bride delighted in the fact that she would not have to do the deep cleaning around the house. Ruth liked her imaginings.

It was not a time for humor. Wen was overwhelmed with grief for his lost rights and the rights of his countrymen. The democratic system's sweeping changes left him yearning for the past, and it was almost too glorious to reclaim. One could not tear an old page from a calendar, one couldn't give experiences away, and one couldn't choose an era of when to live. It was as if one needed to pry one's hands from an hourglass and pull oneself to safety. Safety, Ruth speculated, wasn't top priority. In some hall before an audience, his words and deep sentiment melded into oratory, and he had felt the reaching flame of leadership. The crowd was with him; the people finally understood. He was no rogue or pirate. His voice rose, and when it did, the hearts of men thumped along in harmony.

Ruth awakened with a list of "to do" items on her mind. After breakfast, she called Jim Schnelling about the home improvement plans. Jim had done work for her in he past, and she was comfortable about hiring him. She wanted the library to be accessible from the new rooms and, of course, Wen's family would have a separate entrance. Wen was going to experience full-fledged fatherhood; he was expecting a vibrant family. Three children would provide essential meaning in his private life. Jim recoiled at Ruth's discussion about the perceived agitator and appeared nervous about the old woman's willingness to financially accommodate the man's family. The builder observed that Ruth was treating Wen as if he were a member of her family. Concerned, he offered to call Ruth's minister. Ruth advised Jim not to worry about her and requested quick bids for the construction.

Jim Schnelling and Reverend Phil Boxer visited Ruth the next day. She first explained her building plans to Jim and asked to have a talk with her about her hired hand, Wen Wilson. Phil Boxer thought that Ruth projected her love for her son Daniel onto the political writer. The minister said that the two men were different; her valiant son had given his life to keep the country free, and Wen Wilson was merely an opportunist with a chip on his shoulder over a failed writing career.

"I find it cruel for you to mention Daniel in this way, to suggest that my grief isn't still ongoing and that I don't know my son from a man who has impressed me with his strong beliefs. Wen Wilson has nobody in this world beyond his life at Dan-U Farms, his wife, his child. Now this man has done nobody any harm; he has committed no crime against this town. He is, I'm sure you know, forbidden to write. In my country, it's not a crime to write. In my country, expression is free. You mention my son. Now I mention him. He died for freedoms, and he didn't just die for yours and mine; he died for the rights of men like Wen Wilson."

Phil Boxer smiled gently. His hair was thinning and he combed an unusually long swatch over the balding area. He was average in height and in overall appearance. The minister had no striking feature, and he spoke softly, in a tone that might avert an argument. "We're interested in your safety, Ruth. We're certainly not here to question your grief over your son."

Jim Schnelling entered the conversation. "The addition you're talking about is near the equivalent cost of a house." He looked at Ruth and then the minister. "You're a fine woman, Ruth Uppers. But are you prepared to share your house with a stranger and then finance the expense?"

Ruth shook her head at the question. "I called you, Jim, because you're a builder, and I'm ready to build. Wen and Connie Mae are expecting twins and already have Hugh. I want a business transaction and am not issuing a license to probe into my personal affairs." She looked at her minister. "I hope that I'm known for having a tinge of generosity. No one should interfere with the manner in which I give or how I feel a duty to other human beings." The minister lowered his head as if he conceded on the point. She then turned to Jim. "It's up to you. Do you want to bid on the project or should I call another outfit?" Ruth asked.

"You're putting me on the spot," Jim replied. He was seated on the couch, and Ruth sat across from him in a chair. The living room was the place for formal meetings. "I don't think you know how much people are talking about him, and for you, Ruth Uppers, to become so closely involved with him." Jim paused. "Well, you need to know that people are shocked and are saying you're not in your right mind." Jim waited for the minister to back him up.

"It's true," the minister confirmed.

Ruth assumed the men's uprightness, their propensity to fairness. "What has he done? That is the question that perplexes me when I hear of the talk and disdain for this man. Have you met him? Have you talked to him? Have you read his writing? I assure you he's no more than a man of ideas, traditional ideas about our values as a country. He's neither a spy nor a huckster" Ruth felt a display of passion, and she wished that she had remained more calm. She evened her words and the feeling behind them. "Jim, do you want to bid on the job?"

"I could use the work," Jim Schnelling replied. Ruth was beeped on her walkie-talkie. Mix reported a problem in the North pasture, the field that confined the bull. Galliwag and Wen were fighting. Mix advised Ruth to come quickly. The men naturally followed Ruth to the place of the scuffle; they could not see how Ruth could stop the clash. Two trucks went to the North field, and when the peace-keeping party arrived, Wen was on his back near the fence, trying to catch his breath. Galliwag kicked dirt into Wen's face as a final gesture.

"Mike!" the minister addressed Galliwag. The minister went between the fence wires and entered the field. Galliwag walked in circles, exhausted from his victory. "What's going on?" the minister said.

Galliwag huffed and said as if to the air. "I said I was going to kick his ass." He elevated his voice. "I'm going to kick it again and again until that sissy, book-loving bastard goes away." The minister walked over to Wen, who was still on his back. Jim Schnelling was also standing beside the beaten man.

"Galliwag, I want to see you at the house. Get yourself together and drive over there now," Ruth said. Wen was now sitting up. Ruth walked over to him, and offered him her hand. He stood and was surrounded by three men, Mix, the minister, and the builder. He rose into the gathered circle.

"A nasty fight," Mix said.

"A shame," the minister said.

"I've got a crew of men who feel exactly like Galliwag," Jim said. "Cities are better for bookish men," he added.

"Okay?" Ruth looked at her dusty and bruised friend. She brushed off his shirt and with a finger outlined the injury around his eye. "You're going to lose your good looks if you don't stay away from that man," Ruth told Wen. "I've told you again and again to keep a distance from him."

"I was helping him with a bull," Wen said.

Ruth thought that Galliwag and the bull were a special kinship, heavy, muscular, warring. David Paul drove Connie Mae and Hugh to the site. Connie comforted Wen now, so Ruth motioned for the minister and the builder to come along with her. "You see, Wen needs to be separated from the other hired hands. I'll not have him brutalized because he is different."

"You can't protect him, Ruth," the minister said.

Ruth turned to Jim Schnelling. "If you have a crew of Galliwags, then I'm better off for knowing. Turn in your bid, but I'll increase security at Dan-U Farms." The builder raised his eyebrows, expressing surprise at Ruth's resolute plans. With those words, she planned to let Galliwag go. She decided to sell the noisy ATVs and hire men who could patrol the farm and move cattle on horseback. "If ever you enter into a conversation with townspeople, and they mention Wen Wilson, assure them that I will protect him the best that I'm able. I've given him refuge on Dan-U Farms, and this will be his family's home as long as he wants."

The minister picked up Wen's mangled wire-rimmed glasses and handed them to Ruth. The broken item signaled peril; there were a thousand brutes to every thinking man. The minister witnessed Wen's vulnerability. His religious beliefs wouldn't approve of a beating. Ruth directed her uncertainty squarely to the minister. "Can I count on you to be with us on Sunday?" The minister appeared confused. "Mr. Wilson and his family will join our congregation," Ruth said. "I trust that you'll make sure that he's welcomed in a Christian way."

"The talk," the minister said.

"The talk is talk, Phil, and you shouldn't let it bother you in the slightest," Ruth said.

"I'll give you the numbers on the addition in a couple days," said Jim Schnelling.

"Maybe, I can come out again some time this week, and we can really talk, Ruth," said the minister. The builder put his truck into gear and gravel rose like a billowy cloud in the air. They were gone. Connie Mae escorted Wen to David Paul's truck. Mix was out in the field with the bull. Ruth assumed that she had to deal with Galliwag and so suggested that the Dan-U Farms hired help wait outside the house until her task was done.

Ruth went past the farm's parking areas and pulled her truck into the grass near the side porch. Galliwag was sitting on the wooden steps, looking like a pouting giant, too large for the step's plank and uncomfortable. "I can't have my workers involved in fist fights," Ruth said as she approached the hired hand. "You've dogged Wen since he came here; you've threatened him, tried to intimidate him. What did he do to you?"

"I don't like him," Galliwag said.

"What, the color of his hair, the way he walks, what he says at the breakfast table?" Ruth said.

"He's not a cattleman. He doesn't fit," Galliwag said.

"Well Mike, unfortunately we've had this conversation before. At that time, I explained to you that Wen was a permanent hire, that he had a job at Dan-U Farms. I don't believe that I need to consult with you about my employees, and I won't have you beating them. Come inside. I'll write you a check for two weeks wages." Galliwag stood and waited as Ruth put the key into the house lock. "I'm going to let you go, and I'm sorry about that."

"Your husband wouldn't let a guy like him on the farm," Galliwag said.

"My husband is dead," Ruth said, as she ripped a check from her checkbook. "If you need help moving your things from the men's house, ask David Paul. I'd like you out as soon as possible; also I need your keys to the gates and the outbuildings." Galliwag was beginning to understand the finality of Ruth's decision. He threw a ring of keys on the table. Ruth picked up the key ring and examined individual keys. "It looks like they're all here."

Galliwag paced in a half circle at the table. "Nobody likes that man, and I was holding back. I'll make him cockeyed. He'll be in town some day, and he just won't come back. I'll make that pretty boy bleed, and you know what?" Galliwag said. "The town will cheer for me; they'll make me out as a hero, because there isn't any place for him. He's a sissy-assed poet, and he writes bad things about the country. I know about him. Yes, I do. I do know about him."

Ruth heard David Paul's truck, which meant that Wen, Connie Mae, Hugh and Mix were back. "David Paul is outside. Why don't you talk to him about moving your things?"

Galliwag pointed his index finger at Ruth but was at a loss for what to say. He now paced with his arms extended over his head as if he were going to tackle someone. "It's time to go, Galliwag," Ruth said. His body was bent forward, and he ran from the kitchen. The porch door slammed. Ruth heard words exchanged, but when she looked out, she saw that Galliwag had passed Wen, and he and his family were on their way inside. Ruth greeted them, enfolding the threesome into her arms. Connie Mae held Hugh so it wasn't an impossible physical stretch. "Galliwag is gone." Ruth paused. "With that alone, the tension around the farm will lessen." She bagged ice cubes from the freezer and gave it to Wen for his eye.

Hired Hands

Connie Mae was crying now even while she had been stoic in public. She put Hugh down, and the wife seemed to crawl up Wen's shirt until her face was against his temple. "They're never going to leave us alone," she said. "Galliwag knows people, the wrong people in town," Connie Mae said in what was a cross between whining and words. "He's a mean man," she sobbed.

"The world is full of mean people," Ruth said, and the declaration surprised her. Ruth had meant to comfort Connie Mae, and she was not sure she had offered consolation to the young bride.

"You need to be braver," Wen said to his wife. "A couple blows aren't going to kill me; it hurts like hell though," he chuckled. "I've been put on the ground more than once, I'm not much of a fighter," Wen said. "I told you in the beginning that you weren't marrying a popular guy."

Connie Mae became indignant. "Why do you want to write books that make folks come after you? What do the books say? Maybe you should explain to me just why people are so mad.

It's crazy. It's so crazy. Nobody's words are that threatening; who thinks words are so powerful?" Connie Mae said. She wiped her eyes and noted Hugh's location; the toddler was playing with the drawstring of the window's blinds. "Writers aren't villains. You're not a villain," she told her husband and began crying again.

"With Galliwag gone, I'm going to hire new men. I plan to put together a 24-hour security team who will patrol the farm on horseback. I'm thinking three, and David Paul works well with Lilly. I'm going to install an electronic security gate, and so nobody will be able to enter the farm without first calling up to the house" Connie Mae seemed more relaxed. "And Wen is going to start his next manuscript. I know that that is forbidden, but it is unjust to silence thinkers." Connie Mae squealed in a new panic. Wen rubbed her leg. "We can't be afraid," Ruth said.

Hugh ran to Mix when he entered the room, and the grandfather raised the child in the air. "Hear that?" he said to Ruth. Ruth looked to him. "Galliwag's moving his things; every other piece of furniture hits the ground before it lands in the truck's bed. He's just throwing things." Ruth shook her head. "I've moved the bull to the barn," Mix said and then turned to Wen. "You've taken a hit," he pointed to Wen's eye. "I'll be glad to see him go; I will," Mix said. "Ought to help him pile his stuff on the truck faster, we'd get him outta here. What cha crying about, honey?" Mix put Hugh down on the hardwood floor and went to his daughter. Connie Mae clung to Wen and was silent now. Mix put up his hands, "I'm not interfering. Guess sometimes a girl has to cry for her own reasons. He's not so hurt," Mix said to the young wife. "I've seen men in worse shape," Mix said after examining Wen.

"I'm fine," Wen said. A truck roared out into the gravel lane. Ruth went to the window and saw that Galliwag had left. She went outside and headed towards the men's house. A broken ceramic lamp marked the trail to the dormitory-like building. Its broken pieces appeared like pastel flower petals scattered along on the ground. A soft card table was punctured and was leaning against the house's siding. She knocked at the door. David Paul answered.

He opened the door. "Whew, Mrs. Ruth, ole Galliwag is hot. I reckon he's bound for a drunk tonight."

"He won't be back here," Ruth said.

"He worked for you before the mister died. I'll tell you he got Wen on his mind and couldn't get him off. He'd swear and yell threats to him even when nobody was in the room," the young hired hand said. David Paul led Ruth to Galliwag's emptied part of the house. A chair was tipped over on the floor, and papers littered the carpeting. Loose coins were here and there, a penny, a quarter. Galliwag had left an unscathed framed picture of a wedding; Ruth assumed that it was his first marriage, and she noted his full smile. "Wen never bothers me," David Paul said. "He's just a guy, a little hard to understand at times. Galliwag hated his big words," David Paul paused. "But I don't think Wen uses them to sound smarter than everybody else; he just is smarter than most. Funny, him on a farm," said David Paul.

"We're going to have some new hires; horsemen are going to patrol the farm along the fences." She turned to her employee. "I need bedrooms cleaned and painted for three more men. The horsemen will need to be over six foot tall; they will carry walkie-talkies, no guns. The horses will come from St. Louis so the old stalls need to be cleaned out in the barn." Ruth said. "Wen and his family will stay at the main house. Mix will oversee the men's house."

"Are you afraid of Galliwag?" David Paul asked.

"The horsemen aren't for Galliwag, but for Galliwag types. Cattle rustlers aren't unheard of, and we're not taking any chances with the livestock or the safety of the people who're here. Connie Mae is expecting twins." David Paul smiled. "She needs a safe place for the children," Ruth said. Ruth bent over and picked up a shiny rectangle; it was a link for a watch band. She tossed it in the air and caught it. She observed a picture of Mix standing beside an airplane; it was hanging on the wall. "I had almost forgotten about Mr. Uppers' airplane. One of these days, we should walk up to the garage and see if it still flies. Mix flew it," Ruth said. "Well, be sure to lock your doors tonight, and change your locks after breakfast.

"See you in the morning, Mrs. Ruth," David Paul said.

Her late husband's twin engine was at the center of her dreams. She saw a field of books, some stacked like pyramids but others mostly strewn about, the scene from the library on a large scale. The plane maneuvered through the sky as if the sunlight made it captive, as if it were unable to break through the barrier. The ground could serve as no runway; books covered all spaces. The pilot, who was unnamed but a silhouetted figure, steered the twin engine to a clear gate-like spot in the heavens. Yet on the first approach, it was solid like glass. The propellers rhythmically struck the hard air and were not damaged. The ardent pilot made another advance, determined to break through the invisible obstacle with more precise navigation. The propellers made a grinding sound and sparks hurled upward and all around.

Finally the plane was nearly vertical in flight and ice-like chunks floated around the aircraft; the pieces were iridescent and contained the colors of the rainbow. When Ruth awakened, her hand was holding the bottom of a lace curtain from the window beside her bed. The white lace's pattern was pronounced to her and was more exquisite than she had ever seen. She could hear Connie Mae already at work in the kitchen. Today, she would call the St. Louis Post-Dispatch and advertise for the equestrians.

Ruth was surprised to find that most of the true horsemen she interviewed wanted to bring their own horses. From the newspaper ad, she received responses from seven state counties and one from Taylorsville, Kentucky. She had no doubt that the men from near Kentucky were good horsemen, but could they drive cattle? She also wondered whether or not they were spirited enough to provide security for the farm. She admitted her bias for Missouri men; it seemed they had a good stubborn streak and were determined to act decisively.

She hired Ray Caro, Jason Piny, and Lester Grimes. Ray was a former rodeo rider. Jason had served in the military, and Lester was a hand from a farm in an Eastern county. Mix was put in charge of training the men, of showing them the borders, and of helping the new hires settle into the men's house. A more impersonal employer-employee bond was in order, and Ruth decided to discontinue daily breakfast at her table. Instead, David Paul was paid extra to ensure that a simple meal was on the table at the men's house at 7:30 AM. Ruth and Connie Mae still made breakfast for Wen, Mix, and Hugh.

It seemed that all things were going along as planned. Jim Schnelling, the builder, had dropped off blueprints for the main house's addition. She needed to approve them and free up some money from various investments. Connie Mae was healthy, and the doctor was pleased by the growth of her unborn twins. Wen spent a lot of time in the library and often was seemingly lost in an abstraction. Ruth had given him permission to write, was in the process of providing a comfortable haven for him, as much as it was possible.

The horsemen, being above average height and weight, were available to Wen or Connie Mae if they wanted to go into town. Ruth had explained to the new hires that their jobs meant giving differing types of security, and she encouraged them not to ask needless questions about specific tasks.

Ruth put off Reverend Phil's offer to visit for nearly a month. Of course, she saw the minister in church, but always smiled fully and passed with her hand to the next person she knew. Today, it seemed that Phil insisted on coming out to the farm after church. Ruth dreaded the visit; she did not want to engage in an ethical debate about keeping Wen and his family. While her memories were sweet, she did not want to talk about Daniel or her perceived senility for confusing Wen with blood. Ruth did not want to defend Wen's honor or his patriotism. In fact, since Galliwag was gone, heaviness had left, and Ruth was determined that no man should shame the residents of Dan-U Farms again if she could help it. Her neighbors, no matter how kind their intentions, were into something they couldn't possibly understand because the historical moment had not yet revealed its particulars.

Ruth met the minister at his car, and she decided that they should go for a walk across the lawn.

"Thanks for having me out," the minister said while trying to keep up with Ruth's stride.

"You're welcome here," Ruth said. She watched her step; the action seemed to pull her forward. "I don't think you've ever been out long enough to see the whole of Dan-U Farms." She turned her face to him. "We can walk for a while, or I can drive you in my truck."

"I'd love to see your place some time, but right now we've got to talk. Could we go inside and sit down," the minister said.

"Phil, if you came out to talk about Wen Wilson, I feel I can be frank if I say that that conversation is exhausted." She faced the minister again, smiling, trying to be cordial.

"Actually Ruth, your attorney Paul Davis has been in an automobile accident; he lost control of his car where the creek was running over the highway, and he has now lost consciousness and is in a coma."

"I'm sorry. Is there anything I can do for him or for his family?"

"It's a waiting game, and of course, there's a possibility that Sharleen will need support in the event that they decide there's little hope," the minister said. But I'm here because Paul's last actions before losing control of the car are puzzling. He tried to phone you, and kept telling the ambulance attendant that they had taken his key. Ruth headed to the house to check her answering machine; the minister followed behind her. She reached the phone, and there were messages, two, and both from Paul Davis.

The first message played: "Ruth, Paul Davis. I'm coming out. Maybe Wen Wilson can tell me what's going on now. They've taken my key." The second message played: "I won't be able to make it tonight, Ruth; something's come up with the family. We'll talk later."

"Sharleen said he called and was going to Dan-U Farms and to hold dinner," the minister said.

"Wen," Ruth called. Wen entered the kitchen, wearing baggy jeans and a flannel shirt. He squinted from the light and from not wearing his eyeglasses. "Wen, these messages are from my lawyer, who this afternoon has been critically injured in a one-car accident; he's fighting for his life." Ruth played the messages, and notably watched Wen's face when the key was mentioned. Wen was emotionless. If he knew anything or if he was going to tell anything, it was not evident to Ruth. Ruth thought she understood the key business, but, really, how was it explained to a minister who had not experienced the new system or its corruption?

"Police found this book in the glove compartment." Reverend Phil handed Wen a copy of his book, "Systems." Ruth shuddered; the Canadian distributor had made the book available in the United States. Wen pulled a chair out from the kitchen table and sat. "Do you know why Paul Davis, a well respected lawyer, would have an interest in your banned writing?" the minister asked.

Wen ran his hand through his black hair several times before answering. "The book deals with the legal system and its state under the new anti-intellectualism. It's been a system under fire and has changed dramatically in recent years." Wen looked to Ruth; how much should he say? Ruth sensed Wen's questions; was the man trustworthy; was he sent here in lieu of the police? "He says they took his key. I'd assume that he was denied a pass to practice in some way."

"Then you think the key was metaphorical?" the minister said.

"It's hard to say," Wen replied. "I met the man once and am not familiar with his speech habits. Attorneys are usually quite literal and not poetic. I'd guess that an actual key was taken," the writer surmised. The minister folded his hands and puckered his lips like he might be applying lipstick; the gesture was meant to suggest his deep deliberation on the men's brief but significant relationship. Phil Boxer closed his eyes and appeared to be in a meditative state. The minister opened his eyes after a long while, and he was calm and ready to confront Wen.

"Since you say you only met him once, why would he want to talk to you about a stolen key?" the minister asked.

"You're assuming that I know a lot. My critique of the legal system is in my book, and it is difficult to paraphrase at a kitchen table. It is also too difficult to tell you the thoughts in Paul Davis' mind when he tried to reach us. Your profession also will be reviewed as conduit of intellectual ideas. So far, the church has been spared dramatic revision, though I believe it's probably next."

"By whom?" the minister lightly scoffed at Wen's prediction.

"The U.S. Bureau of Culture," Wen replied. "Ever see the two agents who sit in the second pew every Sunday at your church?"

"Why, that department deals with art, paintings, music, and sculpture," the minister said.

"That department deals with law and language, and whoever uses these functions in our society is suspect. The functions are reinterpreted, made different, and severed from their traditions," Wen told the reverend. The minister began to stand, partly from nervousness.

He paced until he reached the sink. Ruth poured him cold water from the refrigerator; he thanked her. "Put as simply as I know, the target is knowledge, especially knowledge in archives, and that is used as precedents," Wen said. The minister grasped his water glass firmly and lifted it to his lips. "Paul Davis' law books were confiscated and were locked in a room in the courthouse along with other attorneys' books," Wen reported. Reverend Phil audibly sighed.

"The key," the minister said. Wen and Ruth were silent. "I feel like I shouldn't have this information, if it is information. It makes for a compelling story, and I finally realize why the authorities want to silence you. Your stories sound like they're from science fiction. You can't make me believe that this conspiracy hooey is real. It's just crazy, what you're saying," the minister said.

"I assure you, Reverend, that my stories aren't 'hooey' and aren't unsound. If you want proof or want to see with your own eyes, I can show you some pretty unsettling things." Wen now stood and pulled his belt notch a bit tighter. He walked beside the preacher. "I'd be interested to know how Paul Davis is doing." Wen put his hand on Phil's shoulder and then removed it.

"I'll call Sharleen at the hospital." Reverend Phil took out his cell phone and dialed. He waited for an answer. "Yeah Sharleen, this is Phil Boxer. I'm calling to see if there is anything new as far as Paul's condition." He paused. "That's good news. He was awake for a while this afternoon. He knew who you were. He said what?" The minister's face lost its color. "He can't get to his books. He said that several times and fell back into a coma." Phil avoided eye contact with both Wen and Ruth. "I'm praying for you and the kids, Sharleen, and I'm coming to the hospital just as soon as I finish up here. I won't be long."

Ruth took a pot from the oven. "Stay for dinner and take some time to mull over what Wen has told you," Ruth said to the minister. "And once your thoughts have settled, you can go and comfort Paul's wife." She lifted the pot's lid. "A bowl of beef stew and some bread will help you regain your energy." Connie Mae and Hugh entered the kitchen from a bedroom.

"Hey Reverend," she said as she placed Hugh in his highchair. "I heard some of what you're talking about." She turned to Wen. "You never told me all this. You never told me about those men who sit behind us at church. There're agents! I thought it was about your books, now you say it's all books, law, and language." She bent down on one knee and put her arm around Wen's sitting torso. "Honey, I don't know how you know what you know, but you need to stop telling people." Tears rolled down her cheeks. 'They're going to hurt you if you don't," Connie Mae said. "Ruth, God bless her, cannot protect you with three horsemen and a fancy gate. After what you told him today, the minister will walk out on you, the minister," she repeated the word for emphasis. Connie Mae was crying.

"Honey, stop that. I can't tell you anything because your response is always to cry. Yes, this is serious, and we don't know the future. But have you heard the saying, 'the wheels are in motion?' It's too late. I can't turn back. I can't erase what's been written many years ago," Wen said.

"Hush," Ruth said. "Connie Mae, set the dinner table," she commanded. "The minister isn't leaving but is staying for a bowl of stew. Wen, please slice some bread. It's in the pantry. Ruth cut some fresh radishes and green onions." She checked on the quantity of iced tea.

"I'm stunned, I'm shocked by what I've learned," the minister said. "Why, it's all so fantastic."

"It's dangerous," Connie Mae said.

Ruth thought that she preferred Connie Mae's crying to her words. Always at the wrong moment, she was a master of the obvious. Ruth wanted the minister's support. Of course, there was little he could do to change situations, and yet he supplied spiritual solace to a troubled circumstance. "Use cloth napkins," Ruth told Connie Mae. Ruth wanted to bring her into the present moment and away from abstract fears about tomorrow. Mike Galliwag had been too strong and raucous. Connie Mae often reminded Ruth of a flower petal. Their extreme dispositions were both flawed, in Ruth's mind. The elderly woman wanted to deal with neither aggression nor timidity. "After dinner, I'd be happy to go to the hospital with you," Ruth told the minister. Hugh howled because his spoon fell off his tray. Ruth remembered Sharleen's imaginative portrayals of Wen, the foreign spy or door-to door huckster.

"I could go," Wen said. "But I don't want to risk upsetting the family." The minister shook his head and finished chewing his bread before speaking.

"On the contrary, they're aware that Paul tried to contact you, and they don't know what for. I'm asking you to spare the family any of the information that you shared with me. I am certain that in this critical time, it would just confuse them and leave them uneasy and unsure about Paul's professionalism." Reverend Phil swallowed a spoonful of carrot. "If Paul comes to again, he might be able to give his complete message to you. It's a hope," said Reverend Phil. Ruth was inwardly gratified by Phil Boxer's lessening animosity for Wen.

Wen finished his meal, kissed Hugh on the forehead and went to change his clothes. He emerged from the bedroom with blue dress trousers and a white faintly printed shirt. He wore his new eyeglasses because he professed that he could concentrate better with them on. Connie Mae made sharp turns around the table while picking up dishes. Wen knew she was angry about the evening's arrangements. Ruth could see reserve and protective distance in his eyes. Wen disliked arguments with Connie Mae and often pretended to be aloof. Ray Caro and Jason Piny brought the extended cab truck to the side of the house. The two men would escort the group to the hospital in their own vehicle. They would wait outside the intensive care unit. In short, Wen and Ruth Uppers would not be let out of their sight.

The hospital's lighting was too bright and too yellow at the same time. Ruth wondered how bright could be dingy as well. Familiar with the hospital, Reverend Phil led the way to the gravely injured attorney. Ray and Jason were told to hang back from the visiting party, just close enough to detect a disturbance. Ruth could see that Wen was nervous about calling on Paul; he had met him once and remembered the meeting as unpleasant.

The group finally came to the ICU waiting room. Maroon fabric covered ten chairs, and they were in a row along the wall. The minister left the room, and his long absence made it seem like he wouldn't be back. Wen had read all the magazines that interested him and now sat unoccupied. Finally, Reverend Phil Boxer entered the room. "Paul's in and out of it. If you will, follow me," he said. Wen and Ruth stood and went into an ICU room.

Sharleen sat by Paul's bedside, and a ventilator was audible. Wen waited for the right moment and then leaned forward and shook the woman's hand. "I'm Wen Wilson," he said.

"Thank you for coming," she said. She put her clenched fist on her cheek. "He's more conscious but makes less sense. Mr. Wilson, you may try to talk to him if you want. He's fuzzy though." Sharleen Davis moved away from the bedside seat and offered it to Wen.

The writer sat down.

He sat for a moment, unsure of what to do or say. Wen looked up and saw an IV taped onto Paul's hand. He put his hand under the injured man's. Paul squeezed his fingers, and the visitor smiled at the reaction to the touch. "Paul, I'm Wen Wilson. People have been telling me that you want to talk about a key. They took your key, didn't they? Do you know their names?" Paul seemed agitated but only rolled his head from side to side. He mumbled. "Did you tell someone that the key was missing? Who did you tell? Can you tell me a name?"

"Wen Wilson knows," Paul yelled.

"I know, but did you tell someone that we talked about it. Tell me who you talked to about the key?"

"Larry, they've taken my key," Paul said. He shut his eyes, twitched, and faded into sleep.

The minister said, "Stop. You need to take what he volunteers; he's in no condition for the third degree." Sharleen didn't move from the one upholstered chair. She shifted her weight on the vinyl surface. Ruth went to Wen and pulled back on his shoulder, making it clear that she felt his work was done.

"He's been saying that all day. Larry, they've taken my key. The only Larry I know is Larry Gibbons, and he's an attorney in my husband's firm," Sharleen said. "He's one of those lawyers who keep up a license in Florida and in the state of Missouri. He was in town recently but does not live here anymore. I suppose it's possible that Paul could've talked to him on the phone. I'm going to sleep here tonight." She pushed the assistance button and asked for a cot. Ruth helped the attendant arrange the portable bed in the room. Sharleen closed her eyes and began to talk aloud. "God, I don't know how we're going to handle it if you decide to take him. I never figured on this. God, I'm not ready for this." Ruth entered the conversation in her mind, when were people prepared to lose loved ones? It hardly seemed possible; there was no short course on putting one's life back together after loss.

"Larry, please open it for me. They've taken my key," Paul said in a soft voice from a half conscious state.

"Larry, Larry, Larry, I don't understand who he's talking about and why he repeats the same things," Sharleen said.

"Larry Smires is a custodian at the courthouse," the minister said. "He cleans the office at the church after hours. Paul would have known his face, or he might have known him as an acquaintance," Reverend Phil said. Wen looked over to Ruth, showing interest in the minister's information. Wen began to tap his foot as if the added news had somehow upset him and all he knew was to fidget.

"Would this Larry Smires be at the church office now?" Wen asked the minister. Phil checked the time.

The minister surveyed the room, assessing the family's need for him. "Sharleen, I'm going to go with these good people to the church for a minute. Mr. Wilson here seems to think that Larry Smires might be able shed some light on Paul's words. We'll let you rest, and I'll be back in the morning." Sharleen Davis nodded her head;

grasped Reverend Phil's hand and acknowledged Wen and Ruth with gentle eye contact. The worried wife was grateful for the company. The visiting group walked past the waiting room, where they met Ray Caro and Jason Piny. Ray and Jason agreed to follow the threesome over to the church.

The church's dark red brick made the building appear as a great looming shadow, resting on the corner of the town's main street. Phil observed that there were two cars in the parking lot, perhaps left over from the worship services. The minister went to the office's door and turned the key. He stood back and let the others pass. Ray and Jason were the last to enter. Reverend Phil walked quickly down the hall to where a light was on. There was no sign of Larry Smires, but the minister quickly turned to Wen, "Books are missing; this is our library." Ray and Jason bolted down the hallway, turning on lights, checking doorways. "The shelves are empty," Reverend Phil exclaimed. A few books were left on the floor, carelessly opened and turned on end. The minister ran to his personal office and again turned the key. "They're gone; my books are gone," Phil said in almost a panic. "I don't understand this. Who would've done this? Wen Wilson," the minister yelled. He sat on the carpeted floor with his head in his hands. "This is not a joke, this is no minor burglary."

Wen finally found the minister's office. He also sat down on the floor. Ruth stood at the office's entrance. Wen put his arm on the minister's shoulder and listened to the man rage about the strange theft. "What do I do?" he asked Wen. "Do I call the sheriff?" Phil said.

"Yes, call the sheriff. It's what you would do in the case of a burglary," Wen said. Ray and Jason entered the small but comfortable office. Pictures of mission trips hung on the wall. There were two chairs covered in forest green fabric and a clock with a pendulum.

Ray and Jason shook their heads, indicating that there was no sign of forced entry. A key was used, and the thief or thieves had access to the building. Phil picked up the telephone and called Clayborn Burns. The minister then went to stand in the open air; Phil noticed that the cars were no longer in the parking lot. He came back inside. Ruth witnessed that the minister was shaking, as if he were cold; when he raised his hand to secure a push pin on the bulletin board, his hand trembled. He finally sat down in a desk chair with maple armrests.

"Unbelievable," the minister said.

"Not so unbelievable," Clayborn Burns said as he entered the office. "Kids are who you're dealing with; some kids got it in their heads that it'd be funny to clear out your book shelves and so that's what happened." The minister listened and offered no further information, about why the group had come to the church at night in the first place or about the group's visit with Paul Davis in ICU. "You know, I hate to say it, but small towns sometimes bore the teenagers, and they come up with the wildest things to do. I say it's a prank, and the books might return, and they might not. Remember the time some seniors put a Volkswagen frame on top of the high school's roof? You just never know in these cases." The sheriff looked at Ruth and Wen, and noted Ray Caro and Jason Piny in the lobby outside the office. "Dan-U Farms having a meeting at church tonight?"

"These young men, Ruth's employees, Ray Caro and Jason Piny are thinking of joining our church," said Reverend Phil. "I had dinner at the Upper's place tonight, and we wanted to show them the actual church." Ray and Jason briefly squeezed into the office; it was just what they were looking for as far as community. They stepped back into the hallway.

"You know this man?" the sheriff asked the minister about Wen. "Wendell Wilson is on a list of government agitators."

"Oh, I've not heard of that," Reverend Phil said. "I married Wen and Connie Mae Mix and baptized their child Hugh. They come to worship services regularly with Ruth and Connie's dad. I guess I'm not what you call 'politically involved.' I don't have time for it." Ruth knew that Phil Boxer suspected the sheriff's easy answer about the books. Kids rarely messed with texts.

The sheriff walked down to the library, noted the nearly empty shelves. He wrote on a brown clipboard. "Reverend," Clayborn Burns called. When the minister came close, he whispered, "Churches have all kinds, you know, people need the Lord for many reasons; I'm surprised no one has warned you about Mr. Wilson. Some people say he's so smart he's got a screw loose." The sheriff moved his finger in a circle near his head. "He might be your book thief."

"I've been with him all evening," the minister said. He raised his arms over his head and said with authority, "Lord, grant some understanding." He lowered his arms and smiled. "It's in God hands, but I'm sure any help would be appreciated. It's been a long night. I'll delve into this more tomorrow." The minister waited for the sheriff to leave. The minister then sat down and bawled; he cried in front of a solid churchwoman, a known "agitator," and two towering men. Corruption is most unsettling when it's manifested in supposedly trustworthy people. He seemed to stagger into his office, his body leaning in the direction of the room. He opened his desk drawer and removed the Holy Bible. Phil Boxer held it to his chest and tried to regain his breath from sobbing. Ruth recommended that it be kept in a safe.

Ruth motioned to Ray Caro and Jason Piny; she wanted to consult with them about their security plans for both the farm and the church. They followed her outside a door with a heavily varnished finish. It was a solid rectangular piece of wood. The three stood by the brick exterior wall. Ruth was concerned about Reverend Phil; above all he believed in the goodness of his church members, and he could not fathom any conclusion that hinted at an inside job. He was disillusioned to his core and was uncharacteristically suspicious. He did not know who to trust.

A Buick drove around the gravel parking lot, circling near the church's sidewalk and the deliberating group. A pop sounded, and Ruth felt a tug on her sleeve. A fine spray of brick slid down her arm; a bullet had pierced the blouse's fabric, and only missed her arm by the most meager distance. Ray ran after the vehicle, stopping when a misaimed bullet hit a stained glass window. The hired man rolled onto the parking lot as if it were a feathery mattress. When he rose, the loose and sharp rocks had cut into a side of his face. Blood streamed down his cheek in design-like tiers. "The car belongs to the county," Ray said, while he took off his plaid flannel shirt to contain his bleeding wounds.

Ray walked into the church to see the damage to the colorful window. The dove that had rested in Jesus' hand was shattered, and the in-place broken glass gave the bird the appearance of layered wings around the center point of a pencil-thin bullet hole. Ruth now left Ray and went to stick her finger into the bullet-ridden brick beside the church's entrance.

Then she walked to Reverend Phil's office and asked the minister to once again call the police. Phil trembled as he pushed the telephone numbers; he was ready for anything. But the sheriff's deputies treated the second event as vandalism; it was obvious to the law officers that the stained-glass window was the target. Ray tripped over his feet in an ill-advised attempt at heroism. Ruth explained the missing books; she hoped that these latest law men would see the crime from a different perspective. They echoed Clayborn Burns and said that the church was a victim of wayward kids and their antics. Wen laughed aloud, and the deputies glared at him, then they chuckled at him as if to warn him that his time was soon to come.

"The bullets were fired from a county car," Wen said. "I don't think we're dealing with delinquent kids. We're dealing with organized and systematic harassment and theft. Those people responsible knew exactly what they were doing and soon it will out. They cannot do this forever but people will talk." The officers looked at Wen, then one man handed a copy of his report to Reverend Phil. When they passed Wen, the officers came together and pushed their full weight against the writer until he was uplifted and pinned to the plaster wall. One officer removed his gun from his holster and pushed it between Wen's ribcage, and nobody was the wiser. Then they pulled away, and Wen dropped to the floor like a rag doll.

"Ha, ha, ha," the uniformed men said. Ray and Jason moved close to the officers; it was their contracted duty to protect Wen Wilson. Jason threatened to scuffle with one of the deputies. But Wen revived from the fall and ordered the hired men to hold back; he saw no reason for the bodyguards to go to jail, and he predicted that they'd be useful as days went on.

"Overly excitable," Wen said of the hired men. The deputies knew Wen's dilemma and his need to avoid trouble. They hoped for all-out fisticuffs. Ruth sensed that they would not have hesitated to arrest Wen if presented with the right circumstance. Ruth imagined a tearful Connie Mae if she knew the night's happenings. Reverend Phil was cautiously silent, and Ruth suspected he was ready to count his losses; would he explain the missing books to the congregation or remain silent? A good man's tendency toward being closed-lipped was probably standard procedure; what was before one was wrong, and yet, a hundred rationalizations for muted responses invaded the mind. It was easier to be quiet, and perhaps against odds, things would not get worse. Still, Reverend Phil had witnessed what he perceived to be county corruption.

Ray Caro's wounds were cleaned in the main house. Ruth could not leave the nursing task to Mix. It was after midnight when Wen finally met his wife who had fallen asleep on the couch with a pillow and a blanket. Surprisingly, Connie Mae did not awaken to her husband's soft voice. And so Wen sat upright on the floor against the couch's frame. He shut his eyes and rested. The evening's events would not be told; it was just as the police officer said, Ray tripped over his size 14 shoes.

Ruth swabbed his abrasions with a germ-killing ointment. Ruth became aware of the bullet tear on her own sleeve, and she was mildly astonished that fear had not overwhelmed her. Someone had tried to injure or kill her. Ruth watched as Wen stretched out on the carpet. Ruth supposed that the night had too much drama, and the writer didn't dare suggest that his wife move to the bedroom at the present moment.

Ray thanked Ruth, and Ruth offered him a spare cot so the house members might watch over him in case of a concussion. He sheepishly expressed a longing for his own bed and so went to the men's house. After Ray left, she went into her dressing area and examined her arm. But it was the wrinkles on her face that impressed her. Imagine being shot at her age!

Adda's Plight

Ruth felt the coolness of the sheets. The house seemed hot tonight, so warm that Ruth wondered if the furnace had somehow been turned up. The hundred-year-old building creaked, and she listened to water running through the standing radiators. The elderly woman opened her window just a crack and now became aware of nature's noise, the bugs, and the chirping crickets. Before she slept, Ruth was revisited by the disturbing memory on the library's steps; she heard the sound of the police officer's club hitting bone. Adda was pulling on the officer's arm, trying to stop the beating. The man then turned and threw her to the ground and resumed his brutal fit. Ruth knelt beside Adda, who pointed to the victim and cried, "My husband. Please help, find someone to help him."

The officer eventually abandoned the bloodied man; Adda wept because no one would attend her husband. Ruth touched the stranger's wound, and blood was on one of her hands. The young librarian ran down the library's thick stone steps, falling once on account of her foot race away from the violent scene. Of course, she knew that she was due at work, but went at a feline's speed down the sidewalk, bumping into people from her haste.

Adda returned to the library a few days later and told Ruth that her husband died on the operating table; he had massive hemorrhaging in his brain. Ruth discovered at the visit that Adda was pregnant and had five months ahead of her before she gave birth; she was barely showing. Ruth recalled that this was how she met Adda Wilson— not in college. That story was a pretty fabrication and gave away none of Adda's sorrow when she was introduced to Ruth's parents. Rural, church-going Missourians would never understand a woman who was made a widow because of ardent political views. People believed that the status quo, whatever the case, was right and no rabble-rousing was allowed in thought or deed. But Ruth was particularly sympathetic to people who had been left alone, so she sent Adda money, money she could have saved, so Adda could care for her newborn boy.

Ruth paid the hospital expenses for Wen's birth; she later paid for a tonsillectomy and tests for a possible heart condition. Adda seemed unable to closely connect with suitors for a long while; there were marriage offers, but she was unable to imagine her life with anyone other than the child's father. Ruth paid for summer camp, horseback riding instruction, and swimming lessons for the growing boy, all without the child's awareness of her patronage. She financed his first two years of college at the state university, and she took note when he transferred to Brown University on scholarships. Adda's letters mentioned "the boy" and kept her informed of his career as a poet and teacher.

Then Adda became ill, and her lengthy epistles abruptly stopped. Yet, one of her last letters discussed Wen's political writing and his unexpected release from a tenured position at a Midwestern college. Now she felt relieved that the real circumstances had emerged from the depths of her mind. For years she cared for this child-man without a clear rationale for her longstanding consideration. Adda never asked for anything. She didn't complain about her lack of money. Ruth could only surmise that the special and unwilled empathy for the pair was a portion of God's call. This thought comforted her, and Ruth could now sleep.

Ruth awakened to the smell of sausage cooking, and the fact meant that Connie Mae was already in the kitchen. Ruth heard Hugh opening and closing a bottom cabinet door; she showered, dressed, and joined Wen's wife. Connie Mae had breakfast under control, was setting the table. "Late night," she said when her eyes met Ruth's.

"Yes," Ruth said. "Later than we cared for." Ruth watched Connie Mae lift Hugh into his highchair.

"Wen's still sleeping," the wife added. She looked at Ruth. "Ruth, forgive me if I sound ungrateful for what you've done for my family, but well, you can't take Wen out from the farm. I think he's in danger." She paused while putting food on the table. "Forgive me for saying so, but you know he's in danger, and you let him, even want him to go," the tearful wife said.

When Connie sat down, Ruth served the eggs. "I know he's in danger, and you probably should know that there was gunfire last night at the church, and Wen was roughed up by a couple of sheriff's deputies." Connie Mae wailed so loudly that Ruth was sure no one could sleep another minute. "Stop it, just stop it, what good does crying do; it doesn't end the bad situation. It doesn't help Wen when he constantly needs to soothe you when it is his life that's being threatened.

It confuses Hugh to see his mother in tears, so please just stop it."

"You're a hard woman, Ruth Uppers," Connie Mae said in a whining voice. "My daddy says you could walk on tacks, and he's known you forever. I never thought God created such a self-believing heart." Connie Mae became silent when her husband entered and sat down at the table.

"You know about the trouble?" Wen asked Connie Mae. Connie Mae nodded and put butter on Hugh's toast.

"You might as well tell Connie Mae the whole story. I won't have her shocked when she needs to be strong," Ruth said. Connie Mae shook her head as if she was tired of Ruth's call for ruggedness. Ruth stood and phoned Reverend Phil. She asked about Paul Davis' condition. She inquired about the minister's mood, and if he had recovered from the theft of the books. She told the minister that she was visiting Clayborn Burns' house after she finished breakfast; she asked the reverend to join her. "The trouble has started, nobody is starting trouble by asking the sheriff for protection," Ruth said. "Well, sorry about Paul's deteriorated condition, give Sharleen my best thoughts for him, and let me know if you change your mind about going to Clayborn's. Ruth hung up the receiver and said that her lawyer friend was in a deep coma and might be taken off life support machines if he did not improve. She realized that Ray's, Jason's, and Lester's security efforts where of no use if the law itself was the impetus of the persecution. She couldn't consider arming her men, with the system against them. "Reverend Phil is like you, Connie Mae; he imagines and wants desperately to wish the trouble away."

Wen was silent. He had never heard a confrontation between Ruth and his wife. Ruth knew that despite weepy appearances that Connie Mae could hold her own. "Come with me, Connie Mae," Ruth said. "Speak your mind about your worry that Wen is in danger." Ruth took down Connie Mae's sweatshirt from the coat rack. Connie Mae suspiciously accepted the jacket and put it on; she would go.

The two women encountered Clayborn Burns on the sidewalk in front of his home. He was pushing his son in a wheelchair; his only son was stricken with cerebral palsy at birth and was now a young man. Clayborn accepted Ruth and Connie Mae's assistance and moved Kyle onto the porch. The house was still clad in wood siding and was in need of paint in places. The lawn was uneven from infrequent mowing; wild clover covered a portion of a yard. Clayborn was dressed causally and out of uniform; he wore jeans and a golf shirt. "You remember Kyle," he said to his visitors. "Kyle, greet Mrs. Ruth and Connie Mae," he told his son. Kyle waved his arm around his head, and Clayborn smiled at Kyle's way of expression. He sat down in one of the patio chairs and motioned the guests to do so as well. "Why, you seldom drive this route and to this part of town, Mrs. Ruth. What can I help you with?"

"Clayborn, the church last night, you know about the gunshots." Ruth said. "Your men roughed up my hire and held a pistol at his ribcage. Now, Clay I've known your family all of my life. My family was the first to volunteer to take Kyle to a physical therapist in St. Louis. You, Clayborn Burns, were there for my family when Danny was killed. I've known you to be a kind and upright man. I've known you to protect people and observe the law." Kyle dropped a ball that he was hitting against the wheelchair. Clayborn bent over to pick it up and return it to his son. "Call off the local hate campaign against Wen Wilson," Ruth said. He has a legitimate job on my farm, and he has a wife and family," Ruth added.

"You've known Wendell Wilson for a long time, haven't you Ruth? You never went to college with Adda Wilson; she was a graduate of Beloit College, and I know your parents sent all of you to Missouri state schools. Adda Wilson was a member of the Communist Party in her heyday, and I've records sitting on my desk at the office that show that you paid her rent at times, paid for dental care for her boy and so many other things for him. Why? Why Mrs. Ruth would you, the pillar, take up with trashy people for many years?" the sheriff said. Kyle threw the ball and it rolled off the porch and into grass. "Now here's the tragedy; you took him in, and so he has involved himself with a woman who is expecting his babies, I understand." The sheriff paused. "Connie Mae is the innocent one, and if I were you or if you wanted me to offer you some advice, I say get that woman out of there just as fast as you can." He looked at Connie Mae; tears were flowing down her face.

"Why are you doing this to us, Clayborn? Wen is a writer, and no writer's words are so powerful that they should bring on your punishment. The Communists are gone. They're past. I want to raise my children in the same house with their father. Do not blame Wen or Ruth. We've done nothing, and you need to call your people off, and let us live simple lives," Connie Mae said. Clayborn's face began to turn pink and then a bright red, Ruth observed. He stood and went into the house and returned with Wen's latest book. He sat down.

"Connie Mae," the sheriff said, trying to contain his anger. "See this book. Authorities warned your husband about publishing and distributing this book from Canada; he went ahead with it. His life was threatened then, and he didn't take it seriously," Clayborn said. He looked at his son who was silently watching cardinals at a birdfeeder. "Some people would say that Wen Wilson is a genius, because there's no other reason he should know what he knows. Pardon me, now, Connie Mae, but I'm not one of them. He's put Ruth and everyone, including yourself and your children, in danger because he could not stop publishing."

"But the law can protect us; is it a crime to publish?" Connie Mae walked out on the lawn and retrieved Kyle's ball. She handed it to him and sat down again. "Clayborn, you must protect us," the young wife said. "You're elected to do that. We're not spies or agents; we are county citizens."

Clayborn took a laminated card from his wallet. He presented it to Ruth, and Ruth felt fear, a rush of fear. The card was identification for the Federal Bureau of Culture. The sheriff was somehow employed by the larger government agency. Local law enforcement was a part of the national system; Clayborn Burns's allegiances were already spoken for, and he could not help them. "Clayborn, if you needed money, you could've asked. Our families have been friends," Ruth said. He stood at the porch's center entry and ramp. He seemed to survey the neighborhood, how the cars parked along the street, how teenagers left empty coke bottles and beer cans on the grassy strip along the sidewalk. Clayborn Burns shook his head.

"You both think you can save the world, and frankly Mrs. Ruth, that thinking caused all a heap of grief. He thinks he can save the world with pretty words, and you think you can save it also by meeting everyone's unmet obligations. You're a conspirator. Now don't you think that's kind of funny? The queen of Dan-U Farms and Alcott County's good deed doer has aided and abetted a revolutionary and her agitator son a long stretch of her life. Under the new establishment, these are serious crimes," Clayborn said. "They'll not be overlooked."

"If you know part of the story, then you know the whole story. Wen's father was killed in an unprovoked act of violence, and Adda was alone with a newborn child with no means of caring for him." Ruth was becoming angry. "How dare you call me 'a conspirator' for helping a destitute family! How dare you mock my life when you have sold out to thugs and book burners, to men who would steal the libraries of churches as a day's work! I've known you Clayborn, and I've seen you weep like a child when an Angus calf was born with a twisted leg. Where's that humanity? Where's the kindness you showed when my son was brought home? Remember how you let me collapse into your arms and how you stayed with us into the night? Has this 'club' stolen the bread from your soul?" Ruth said.

Clayborn saw three boys on bicycles, and said, "Help me. Quick, help me move my son into the house." The boys waggled as they rode on the sidewalk and then moved out into the street. Clayborn handled the wheelchair with extraordinary roughness. "Please open the door," he said.

"Monkey boy, it's monkey boy, got any bananas, ee, ee, ee," a bicyclist yelled at Kyle as Clayborn rushed him into the house. Ruth followed the sheriff who leaned against a wall as if he were hiding. "Daddy, bring monkey boy out to play, ee, ee, ee. He wants to play with us."

Connie Mae confronted the delinquents. "Shame on you; do you hear me? You're cruel and bad boys. Go away," the woman said. The boys cursed Connie Mae and called her names. Yet, she continued to shame them until they rode down to the end of the block and then out of sight. She gathered her purse from the patio table and went inside. "I'm ready to go, Ruth," she said. A tear slid down Clayborn Burns's cheek. "I'm sorry," she said. "We're going," Connie Mae added. Ruth followed Connie Mae to the vehicle and was unsure if anything was resolved. It surprised the farmwoman that Clayborn Burns knew about Adda's background; databases were increasingly jammed with private facts and detail.

"So Wen's actually has been like your son?" Connie Mae said, as she turned the truck's ignition.

"No, not like my son but a heartfelt interest," Ruth said. "I cared that he was fed, that he had decent clothes and an education. But heavens, I didn't know him except from what Adda reported in letters. I was satisfied when he was doing well and proud of his graduation from Brown," Ruth recalled. "I knew Adda had strong political beliefs; I shied away from her politics and even political discussion. Remember, I witnessed Wen's father's killing for political reasons and wasn't interested in bringing the law my way," she said.

"It looks like Clayborn's past friendships aren't meaningful. My God, what has happened to us?" Connie Mae was going to cry, but Ruth stopped her with a stony glance. "You hate my crying, I know, and I don't mean to do it to bother you, but I don't know what we're going to do or where we're going to be safe. I hardly believe what my ears have heard today," Connie Mae said. She turned the truck and was now on Dan-U lane.

"I don't know what we're going to do either," said Ruth. But we're not going to cry," the farm-woman said.

Reverend Phil, Sharleen Davis, Wen, and Hugh were sitting at the kitchen table when Ruth and Connie Mae entered the house. The minister and Sharleen brought a tape of Paul's unconscious utterances at the hospital; they wanted Ruth to hear a portion where Paul suggested that his car was being chased and squeezed off the road. The accident might have been a premeditated attempt to take Paul's life. Connie Mae, exhausted from her encounter with Clayborn Burns, greeted the visitors and then took Hugh to the back bedroom so that he could go down for a nap. Ruth poured coffee into a canister, and she listened.

"Back off, I tell you. Pass me. I can't drive this road so fast. I'm going to pull off the road," said Paul's recorded voice. Sharleen stood and turned off the machine. She sat down somberly.

"He says those same words over and over, sometimes in a different order. I'm going to call Sheriff Burns, but Reverend Phil wanted you to hear it first, thinking you'd know best what to do," Sharleen said. Ruth filled the coffee cups and was still deep with thought over her conversation with the sheriff and with his revelation about the culture bureau. Ruth was unsure about how much Sharleen knew and so refrained from giving out information. Luckily, Sharleen yawned and expressed a lack of sleep. So after two cups of coffee, Ruth beeped Jason on the walkie-talkie and asked him to drive Sharleen home. "You're just back from Clayborn's house," Sharleen said. "Did he mention Paul's talk about the keys? I told Clayborn about Paul's talk about somebody taking his keys."

"No, No, he said nothing concerning that," Ruth said. Jason gave a slight knock; he came into the kitchen. "Take her home, Jason. Sharleen, we'll talk more after you've rested and after I sort through all the bits and pieces in my mind. We can put Paul's words so that they make sense without Clayborn Burns for a couple of days," Ruth said. Sharleen looked confused.

"You don't want me to call the sheriff?" Sharleen said.

"Who am I to say these things? Do what you feel you must," Ruth replied. "Yes, I suppose you should." Jason waited for Sharleen to gather her things, a silk scarf and a red purse, and she went with him to the door and to his vehicle. Ruth let the top of her thin body collapse on the table, dramatizing her tiredness. She put both hands in her hair and acted as if she were pulling on it. "Phone the sheriff, a lot of good that will do you," Ruth said after she heard Jason's truck go out the lane.

"I don't think cynicism helps, Ruth," Reverend Phil said. Ruth looked at Wen, who was waiting for a report on Ruth's and Connie Mae's visit to the sheriff. She was momentarily impressed with his coal-colored eyes and hair, how a shadowy beard colored his face. Ruth knew that Wen believed the minister was still naive or unwilling to see the part of the picture put before him.

"I've seen his identification card, and Clayborn Burns is an employee of the Federal Culture Bureau," Ruth confirmed. Reverend Phil stood and clasped his hands together, then began pacing in the small space around the kitchen table. "It'll do Sharleen no good to call on him for help," Ruth said.

"He's a law man; he filed on complaint on the church's missing books. No, I'm sure you're mistaken. There's no conspiracy against knowledge in Alcott County, in this little place," the minister laughed. "Sure, it was kids who cleared out our library. No, I just can't believe that local law enforcement would be in collusion with the government's culture agency."

"What about Paul Davis?" Wen asked.

"I don't know. It's possible that he became involved with the wrong people, you know, a vengeance case," Reverend Phil speculated. "Attorneys must meet many types, and types on the wrong side of the law," he added.

Wen pulled up his flannel shirt and revealed a large bruise near his heart. "The deputies' guns that night at the church. I was lifted off the ground with gun metal and dropped on the hard tile. Now, I don't think of that incident as really mattering, except for the fact that I want you to know that appearances aren't reliable anymore. You can't just assume that there is safety where there're police officers. I promise you that your books weren't taken by teenagers. Right now, right here, we all need to think as if there is no public security or protection." Wen paused. "Paul Davis wasn't safe, and so, please know that we aren't either."

"This is nuts, just nuts, a guy's in an accident, some books are missing. What're you suggesting,

Wen, that we go to the local sporting goods store and be vigilant? I'm a minister. I can't go in for this kind of talk, you need to believe the best about human nature," Reverend Phil said. "Besides, I don't believe in guns. I wouldn't own one," he said.

"Nobody wants you to buy a gun. I don't have a gun," Wen said. "Right now, you need to believe what is true. You need to accept the circumstances as they are." Wen pulled out a gold tone watch with a broken band. "Reverend Phil, did you ever see Larry Smires wear a watch?"

"Well, yeah," Reverend Phil said.

"Was it like this?" Wen asked.

Ruth went to her windowsill and retrieved a small broken section for a watchband. "That's Galliwag's watch. I found these links when I was in the men's house, and for some reason didn't throw them away," Ruth said.

"I found the watch in the church's parking lot. Does Mike Galliwag go to your church, Phil?" Wen said.

"No," Reverend Phil replied. "I've seen him with Larry Smires, though. There's a family connection; Mike dates Smires' sister, lives with her or something. I hear so much at the church that I'm not sure what I've heard." Phil finally sat down and forced a smile, as if to suggest that all the negativity had not taken his optimism. And Mike Galliwag might be a thief, but he was not the government or even a likely candidate for a government job.

"A prank, yes, maybe a prank. The guys have a little bit too much to drink, and then they decide to steal the books at the church." Now Wen stood and was obviously nervous; he was getting no where with the minister. Reverend Phil earnestly wanted for everything to be all right.

Ruth noted that Wen was ready to announce that he was going to bed; he couldn't deal with Reverend Phil's denial. Then, surprisingly, Wen sat down again. "Phil, that night at the church, when you discovered the books were missing, you cried, you cried like a man experiencing tremendous loss, like a man whose world was out of control. Tell me, why did you cry like that?" Wen looked directly at the minister, and the minister stood as if he were ready to leave.

Reverend Phil was in front of Ruth, as if he were waiting for something. "Do you want Ray or Lester to follow you home?" Ruth asked. "I know this part of the county seems so isolated at night." Wen now stood; it was obvious that the minister was not going to talk about that night at the church.

"Well, I'm going to bed," Wen said. "We'll talk again," he said to Reverend Phil. The minister nodded, and Wen left the room. Ruth and Reverend Phil heard the bathroom door shut.

The minister lowered his voice to a whisper. "Ruth, pardon me for saying so, I know you're attached to Wen, and he's not a bad guy as I've sat here and talked to him, but you must make him go, you must tell him, maybe give him money, that there's been too much trouble in town since he's been here, and while you personally like him and his family, he needs to find another place to live, a place where nobody has heard of him," Reverend Phil said.

"Not very neighborly, Reverend Phil," Ruth said. "Tonight he was trying to show you that this is bigger than you or me or Alcott County. Is this the classic case of blaming the messenger?" Ruth beeped Lester. "Lester, would you escort Reverend Phil into town for me. I know it's late, but I'd sure appreciate it." Ruth put the walkie-talkie on the table.

There was silence. "Don't be angry," the minister said. "I'm looking for a solution as well as you are."

"Preach on the missing books; stop deserting people, stand up for people and for your church,"

Ruth said. "No, I don't want to hear any more talk about Wen leaving; he has a home with me. I've known of Wen for a long time; I paid for his trumpet lessons when he was in the seventh grade. I bought him a pair of dress shoes for a high school dance. When it comes to Wendell Wilson, you see, I'm a collaborator, a conspirator, a woman who has cared about him."

"I don't understand," the minister said. Lester stuck his head through the door and was waiting. "We'll talk, Ruth. I promise you, we'll talk just where we left off," Reverend Phil said. He looked about the room for anything he might leave behind, and then hurried off with the hired hand.

The door closed. Wen, hearing the minister's exit, returned to the kitchen table wearing pajamas. "I'm sorry. I couldn't sleep and overheard your conversation with the minister."

"Trumpet lessons and dress shoes?" Ruth smiled; their eyes met and exchanged feelings of warmth.

"Time isn't on your side; you need to start another manuscript and finish it. Work on it every day, let Mix and David Paul, and the rest handle the farm work. Sir, cows weren't in your stars," Ruth said. "Clayborn Burns said he's known about me for a long time, about my sympathy for agitators. I guess people might say that Ruth Uppers has always valued her reputation." The elderly woman put her hand on Wen's forearm, and then took it away. "Wen, no man could have caused such a stir if he weren't brilliant. Write the book of your life for me and with the brain that God has given you. You've a great gift."

"Your church will be looking for a new minister," Wen said. "I bet he resigns within the week."

"He's afraid. He knew the truth when he was crying at the church, and he still knows the truth," Ruth said. "Good night, Wen. Ruth shut off the light and retreated to her bed and was quickly asleep.

Ruth awakened with Hugh's hands on her face as if the toddler were sculpting. Hugh giggled when his finger went into Ruth's nostril. "You climbed out of your crib." Ruth said. She checked the clock; it was 6:00 AM. She asked Hugh if he had heard Felix crow yet. "Does your mama take you to the chicken house? The chickens are very still through the night but when the sun shines, the rooster thinks every chick should celebrate, and he crows, 'Cock-a-doodle-doo.'" Hugh laughed and climbed under the blankets. He snuggled against her. She listened to ice drops pelting at the window and was consciously feeling comfortable. Then truck tires sounded on the gravel, and the vehicle was heading to the men's house. She leaned over to her cherry nightstand and picked up the walkie-talkie. "I was wondering if that's you coming in, Jason? Did you take Sharleen Davis home okay?"

"Yeah, it's Jason, Mrs. Ruth. Sharleen was scared and wanted me to spend the night, so I did," the hired hand said.

"You did," Ruth said to confirm that she had heard right. "Jason, Sharleen's husband is in critical condition at the hospital.

"She didn't tell me that, Mrs. Ruth," Jason replied. "I never would've thought that from her conversation," he said.

"I don't need this now," she said. "Meet me at the stables in about a half hour, 7:00 or so," Ruth said.

Ruth put on a pair of worn blue jeans and a darker blue fleece sweatshirt. The toddler was asleep on her bed, and she decided to leave him undisturbed. She went to the bathroom to comb her hair and brush her teeth. Finally, she sat down at the kitchen table with a glass of tomato juice. Within minutes Ruth's movement awakened Connie Mae, and she called out for Hugh.

"Shhhh," Ruth told the mother. Hugh is in Woo's bed. He crawled in bed with me, went back to sleep." Connie Mae smiled. Their visit to Clayborn Burn's home seemed to bond the two women. "I'm going riding with Jason Piny, he's a early bird this morning. I'll be back in a few hours." Connie Mae nodded, went by Ruth bedroom door to check on Hugh and then went back to Wen.

Ruth opened the stable's massive double doors and found Jason sitting against a stall post. His black stallion was in the end stall, far from Lilly and the other horses. He had what Jason called, "a temperament problem" and was anti-social with people and horses alike. Ruth unlocked a cabinet and removed a silver pistol; she tucked into her belt. Her hired hand wanted to know if she anticipated trouble. "I'm learning to anticipate trouble," Ruth said. "Put saddles on Lilly and Black Jack, and let's go for a ride," she instructed Jason. Soon Jason and Ruth were on their horses, and Ruth led to a weed-covered strip at the top of the ridge. "This was my late husband's runway; he'd land his twin engine right here. Jason, I want bulldozers, whatever earth-moving machines are necessary to reopen this landing strip." Ice was falling like rain, and with the foul weather, it seemed like the wrong time to discuss country airports.

Jason rode away from Ruth and followed the once cleared road.

He rode back to his employer. "The strip's in pretty good shape. I'll bring Lester up and see what he says. What's your timeframe, Mrs. Ruth?" Jason said. His horse jumped and danced in place. "I was afraid that you wanted to talk to me about Sharleen Davis. I just didn't know that it was her husband that we went to the hospital for; I'm telling you she almost threw herself at me. I didn't imagine a husband in the picture; that's why I thought you had me take her home."

An Intruder

◡

"Jason, I'm an old woman. I strongly disapprove of the situation, no matter who thought or did whatever." She looked at him sternly. "I don't want to hear your reasons. I don't want excuses, and I certainly don't want to hear what happened between the two of you," Ruth said. The sound of an ATV engine drowned out Ruth's last words; its operator wore a knit face-covering ski mask. The vehicle did not belong to Dan-U Farms, and it steered toward Black Jack. The horse went up on its hind legs, though Jason was able to control it. The ATV passed again, revving the engine when it went by the high strung stallion. This time Jason fell from the horse and was on the ground. The ATV chased Black Jack and drove him away from his rider. Then it circled around and was going to make a pass by Jason. Ruth pulled out her pistol and aimed at the driver's hand, an arm would do. She fired the gun like a marksman, hitting her target. The ATV zigzagged, and the driver held a bloody hand in the air; he drove away, across the fields, and off Dan-U Farms. Ruth checked on

Jason, and then went for the frightened stallion. Ruth returned the horse to its rider. Lilly was as steady as ever. "You okay?" the elderly woman said. Jason was unhurt.

"Who told you to pack that pistol?" Jason said as he regained control of his horse. "They sure spooked Jack."

"Spooked me," Ruth said. Ice had formed on her eyelashes; ice drops were still hitting the ground. She held the cold gun so that it touched Lilly's saddle and was out of sight.

She knew the day was coming when she'd have to fly her adopted friends off the farm to Canada. She thought about Michigan and the Upper Peninsula; it was worthwhile to feel cooler weather.

"I think that driver would've run me over," Jason said. Ruth contacted her hired hands on the walkie-talkie and told them to be on the lookout for ATV intruders who might disturb the livestock. Once back at the house, she had a telephone message from Jim Schnelling who said that the ground was not frozen and the foundation could be dug for the new addition, but there was a hang up with getting a building permit. Jim wanted Ruth to talk to the county office. She now had no need for more space at the main house. She called a St. Louis auctioneer and was going to deliver a herd at the stockyard. Within the calendar year, if possible, she planned to phase out of the cattle business. David Paul was skillful at driving a semi-trailer, and nobody would be called locally or from outside the farm. He could make a delivery. The herd sale was arranged.

Now Ruth telephoned Reverend Phil to check on Paul Davis' condition. The minister explained that the wife decided to take Paul off the life support machines, and he passed away just minutes before Ruth's call; it was a difficult decision. Strangely, while he was more than a mile away from the house, she heard Jason's voice as he tried to move Black Jack back into the stables. Ruth mostly liked her hired hands, but today she was filled with doubt over Jason's unusual encounter with Sharleen. Sharleen's decision to end her husband's life seemed murky in light of Jason's early morning arrival. The combined circumstances bothered her enough that she vowed to push thoughts about them from her mind. She resolved to stay in and to avoid Jason, if possible.

Her pistol was on the table. She stood and dug into her jean pockets for the remaining bullets. Ruth put the bullets into a small metal box on the windowsill and put the gun in a drawer under folded dish towels. She had never run up against lawlessness and had never felt the helplessness of not being able to call the police force. She was alone. For years, Ruth had nurtured the finest participation in community. She was there for her neighbor and members of her church family. Ruth had crafted angels for the chapel's Christmas tree and adorned the altar with stunning bouquets. Ruth Uppers had served on boards and state commissions. She wanted no reward, but she had never imagined being at odds with a system.

She walked into her library, where Wen was busy typing his thoughts. Ruth pressured Wen to finish his next volume, telling him that she didn't know how long she could discourage his enemies. He turned to her with an earnest face. "I fired shots at an intruder today," she told him. "I hit his hand, and the driver almost lost control of the ATV." Wen turned his body in the desk chair and was now facing his elderly patron. "I want to fly you and your family to Canada after you're finished with this manuscript." Ruth said.

Wen began tying a scarf around his head, was bothered by the hair on his forehead. "I thought you said we wouldn't run. You said that running is the worst thing we can do," he said.

"Wen, I wounded someone with a gun today. He was trying to run over Jason Piny, but let's put it this way: violence is coming to us, and its coming to us more frequently. At first I thought you could settle down, do a day's work and raise a family on this farm. I now realize that there is an active conspiracy; it's in motion, and there are people who blame you for knowing about it, for writing about it, for telling others." Ruth smiled at the scholar.

"Mix took Connie Mae and Hugh to the barn to see the birth of a calf," Wen said. "She'll be having our twins soon. Alcott County is her home. I think it might upset her to hear talk about moving. Ruth, you need to think about this long and hard. I can go. After all, I'm the one they want; it's my scalp that will satisfy them. I don't think they'll hurt Connie Mae or the children if they stay, and your life is bound to improve if I'm gone." He began typing.

"I think you need to stick together. You need to be prepared to act in an emergency, say, if we must evacuate Connie Mae and the babies from the farm. And you, what if a mob was at the gate?" Ruth asked.

He stopped typing. "If a mob shows up at your gate, I'll walk out there and turn myself over to them," Wen said.

"You'll never make it to trial; it'll be vigilante justice, and who knows if they'll stop at you." Ruth was frustrated. "Wen, I don't know how you see yourself, as a writer, as a reformer, as an activist; they see you as a revolutionary, and if they take you, you won't see the walls of a cell. You're a husband and a father, and you must make your family a priority. For you even to think of some kind of martyrdom is selfish. I won't let you go without them. Children without fathers are no better than orphans and are subject to the world's licks."

"Is that why you sent my mother money?" Wen asked. "I always knew that there was a good fairy in my life, eyeglasses appeared even after my mother fended off bill collectors and small claims court judgments." A tear swelled in his eye. "If I hadn't eyeglasses, I'd not been able to read. Every early picture of me shows a squinty-eyed kid in mismatched clothes," he laughed.

"Paul Davis is dead," Ruth said. "Sharleen had the ventilator stopped and whatever else kept him alive."

"He was run off the road, I think, because he wanted to talk to me," Wen said. "How is the wife doing?"

"Okay, I guess," Ruth said. She would say nothing about Jason and his visit to the Davis home. Even if she wanted to gossip, she couldn't repeat the ugliness. It was too much. Wen seemed bound within a scholarly cocoon, and she felt unable to communicate with him about real danger. He'd been bounced on the ground, spat upon, threatened with the deputy's gun. Indeed, Ruth was beginning to think that he believed in good fairies more than the existence of a dark side of human nature, and that despite all, he would have an access to eyeglasses or whatever he lacked. It was as if he thought that a protective aura surrounded his being, and somehow it extended to his family. Throughout all, he hadn't asked for a gun.

"Why don't you carry a gun?" Ruth said.

Wen stood and went to the front of the desk. He acted as if he were thinking about Ruth's question. "Hmmm," he said. "I don't know how to use a gun, for one thing," he laughed. "But in all seriousness, I don't think I'd be alive today if I had picked up a gun. I would have been the 'outlaw,' and there's no one who's going to blame someone who goes up against an outlaw."

Wen's fingers went over the ornate carvings in the desk, of wheat and peasant farmers. "I think your day has come, Mr. Wilson," Ruth said. "Believe it or not, publishing that last book and distributing it through Canadian channels has made you a bona fide outlaw, and I don't think anyone cares if you're unarmed; they didn't care if Paul Davis was carrying a weapon," Ruth said. "I want you to finish the current manuscript as fast as you can and learn to use a gun."

"No, I can't use a gun. I won't resort to counter-violence," Wen said. "I won't become what they want me to be." Wen shut an opened book, signaling that he was done with the source and with the conversation.

"I find your extreme sense of self appalling," Ruth said before she had considered and tempered her words. "I'm sorry," she said immediately. "It bothers me when you think so much of purity and the purity of your cause. I'll put up a secure home for your family out of the country or wherever you want to go. I was thinking of buying a house in the Upper Peninsula. It's secluded, and I believe your wife and children will be safe. Connie Mae is welcome to invite Mix. You can continue your writings." Wen sighed. "Would you accept this plan in an emergency?" Ruth asked Wen, growing angry at his theory-based world.

"Are you running us off Dan-U Farms?" Wen said, as he returned to the desk chair and sat down.

"I'm closing Dan-U Farms. I want to go with you if you'll have me," Ruth said. "I'm fond of your family." Wen smiled and nodded as if Ruth would be welcomed to join the group.

"That's why you must learn to use a gun, not for some use against the opposition, and I don't want you thinking that it's wrong from a public principle, but Wen, the day might come when you need to fight, really fight, not out of meanness but out of your obligation, hear me now, out of your absolute duty to defend your loved ones." The library doors opened, and Connie Mae and Hugh entered. Hugh put his hands on his hips and ran around the room as if he were flying and yet wingless. He stopped when he came to Ruth.

"Woo, we see calf and stand on legs," Hugh said. He could hardly contain his excitement. Connie Mae looked tired from standing on her feet; the doctors said she'd deliver twins within the month. She put her hand on Wen's shoulder and assessed the available chairs in the room. She chose a peach-colored upholstered club chair. Hugh immediately sat on the floor near her.

"You missed the miracle of life," she told Wen. The cow gives birth by itself; Daddy helped a little with this last one. I don't know why you didn't come down to the barn. I was looking for you. I thought you'd take a break," Connie Mae said. She rubbed the armrest.

Her words registered as a complaint to Wen. "I'm not throwing bales of hay; I can't easily pick up where I left off," Wen said. Connie Mae was silent. She reminded herself that Wen wasn't a farm hand; he was a writer, and he seemed peevish to the pregnant wife.

"Just a few minutes ago, the Upper's barn was the place to be in Alcott County," Connie Mae said. Daddy, David Paul, Jason, Lester, Ray, Hugh, Reverend Phil, and Sharleen Davis were waiting for this clumsy calf to be born. I was there, so that's one more added to the crowd."

"Why is Sharleen Davis here?" Ruth asked. "Her husband is just hours dead, and she's hanging out at a cattle barn."

"Yeah, it's too bad about Paul. Sharleen said she couldn't stand to see him on the support machines and had to let him go. Doctors held out slim chance for his recovery," said Wen's wife.

"I reckon Sharleen will come in with the minister and state her business," Connie Mae said. She was satisfied to share the latest news and to have been the first to talk to Sharleen Davis. "I do know that Sharleen said that she was jittery and wanted Jason Piny to stay over for a couple of days," Connie Mae said and then smiled. "She is sweet on Jason Piny; I can tell by the way she looks at him." Ruth frowned at Connie Mae. Wen began putting away his books because of the visitors; he'd finish up on his work for the night and quit writing. The books went into the shelves like slices of toast.

"Don't bother yourself with gossip, Connie Mae," Ruth said. "You must be mistaken about what Sharleen wanted." Connie Mae put her lips together tightly and shook her head as if she were a rebellious child. Ruth could see that Connie had a mind about Jason and Sharleen.

"Her fingernails are painted red, the same color of her lips. She's wearing a short, tight-fitting skirt, what is she, 50 or something, and it's cold out there, the ice has been falling all day," Connie Mae said. "She isn't trying to show off for Daddy or Reverend Phil," the woman concluded.

Mix beeped Ruth on the walkie-talkie. "I'm bringing the Reverend and Mrs. Davis into the house, wanted to let you know." Wen began shooing the group from the library. Ruth wondered why Reverend Phil and Sharleen Davis had gone to the barn first. Connie Mae put Hugh down in his crib, and the makeshift family went to the kitchen to greet visitors.

Mix led the minister and the new widow into the room. Ruth extended her arms, folding them around Sharleen.

"I'm sorry, dear," Ruth said. "Paul was a good man, kind, charitable, professional. I'm able to say so much about him, and how he cared for others." Ruth held Sharleen back at arms' length so she could see her face and have eye contact with her. Ruth was surprised to see eye make-up streaming down her cheeks in tears. Sharleen pulled close to the older woman.

Connie Mae caught Ruth's view of the cosmetics and inwardly laughed at her shock, and then she went to the refrigerator and spread out a cold chunk of country ham. She also put out bread, mustard and mayonnaise for sandwiches. Ruth reminded Connie Mae about a container of potato salad. The "bringing out of food" interruption annoyed Sharleen, and she tightened her embrace and began audibly sobbing. Reverend Phil made a sandwich.

"Ruth, Ruuuth," Sharleen wailed. "I don't know how I'll do it. He did so much, and I'm alone." Mix gave her a tissue, and he was solemn, perhaps remembering his own losses.

Wen went close to the mournful widow, and Connie Mae gently nudged her husband and warned him to keep his distance from her. "Now, Reverend Phil is going on sabbatical; I will have no one," Sharleen reported. Wen smiled at Ruth and was proud of the accuracy of his prediction: the minister wouldn't stay.

"A monastery in Italy," Reverend Phil said. "It's a place to deepen my spirituality. I can grow," he added. Wen cut off a slice of ham, eating small pieces as a seeming theater went on before him.

"A sudden decision?" Wen said.

"No, no, these retreats are planned months in advance. It happens that a good friend of mine wasn't up for his scheduled stay at the monastery, so I'm filling in for him with the permission of the presbytery," Reverend Phil said. Sharleen was crying louder now, and Connie Mae feared that the noise might awaken Hugh, who would be flustered by such a dramatic situation.

"I've heard of your close call this morning," Sharleen said. "I don't know how I'll feel safe."

"Well Sharleen, you've heard that I'm a sharp-shooter, and I don't mind at all staying with you tonight. Let me grab a few things, throw them into a bag, and we can go into town to your house," Ruth said. Sharleen was startled, without words. Connie Mae said she'd see about Hugh. "I've never bragged about it, never thought it was lady-like... I'm fine with a gun though."

Sharleen was suddenly recovered from her shaken state. "Ruth, that's too much. I can't ask so much of you. You've a farm, a new calf, and just more work than I can imagine. I will be fine. The grief is fresh," Sharleen whispered. "I'll get over it in time," the widow said.

"If a woman's protection doesn't appeal to you, Sharleen, I mean maybe you wouldn't feel so safe with me. I could send you one of my boys, to sleep on the screened-in porch," Ruth said. "Connie Mae's daddy is another sure shot with a pistol, and I've no doubt that Mix would keep you out of harm's way." Sharleen was nervous about the idea of sending the old hired hand to her home. His facial skin was severely wrinkled and put into mind an exotic pedigree dog.

Connie Mae entered the room with Hugh, and she smiled at Ruth's suggestion to send Mix home with Sharleen Davis. Sharleen sensed

Connie Mae's amusement since they were together in the barn when the new widow asked about Jason Piny's availability for a few nights. "Oh Ruth," Sharleen said, "I can't take your employees, it is wrong to be so self-centered." She turned to the minister, "I think we should be going. I don't want to be on a county road after dark." Reverend Phil thanked Ruth for her generosity in putting out the food.

Ruth's voice was gentle and resigned to Reverend Phil's flight from Alcott County. She fantasized about the possibility of going into spiritual cloister herself. "When are you leaving for Italy?" she asked. Ruth pictured the minister in robes, tending lush gardens and preparing community meals, creating stews filled with homegrown vegetables and herbs.

"Next week, after Paul's funeral," the minister said. Wen was amazed over the news of his quick exodus. Ruth noted that Wen's eyes registered mischievousness, and she doubted that he'd let Reverend Phil off the hook.

"What's the hurry?" Wen asked. Reverend Phil ignored Wen's question, informing Sharleen that he was ready to go. Wen stood up and walked out the outside door. Ruth heard him begin to split wood for the woodstove. The hammer fell on the wedge at a furious pace; the strong hit of metal against metal sounded in the kitchen, making the exiting visitors tense.

"Wen Wilson is moody, isn't he?" asked Sharleen. Sharleen and the minister expressed their gratitude once again for the sandwiches and then made their way to the door. Wen continued to pound on the wedge. After the guests had left, the frustrated activist brought in an armload of wood. Pieces of bark fell on the light-colored carpeting, marking a trail across the room. Wen stacked the split logs beside the stove, putting the choicest logs in the fire.

"I knew Reverend Phil wouldn't stay," Wen said bitterly. "I guess the guy had as much truth as he could handle." Wen leaned back and watched the flames through the stove's window. Mix sat down in a floral-design upholstered chair and began to doze off with Hugh on his lap; the toddler was also near sleep. Connie Mae sat beside Wen; the unborn twins were calm and did not stir in their mother's womb. Ruth contemplated the strange day from a favorite recliner. The elderly woman was not prone to introspection, and yet she wondered why she was still surprised at the shadowy quirkiness of human nature; it was certainly time for her to stop being disillusioned at every odd and indecorous move.

She moved quietly into her bathroom, pulling the curtain back to see if Jason's truck was in the lot. It was, and Ruth was relieved, and so she washed her face, brushed her teeth, and immediately went to bed. Ruth dreamed of miniskirts, polished nails, and modern symbols of enticement. In between fiction and theatrics, she fervently tried to remember what Wen's answers had been; did he agree to move with his family in an emergency or to carry a gun? Her sleep was restless, deep, and then restless again. At 9:30 AM, Ruth rose. She resolved that this would be a day of business; she would contact a respected airplane mechanic to make sure the Cessna was in sound order and arrange for heavy equipment to revamp the runway. After these tasks were done, she decided to drive to the court house, mostly from curiosity, to check on the status of her building permit. She showered and combed her short and wiry gray hair. She put on a pair of black slacks in lieu of a dress; the weather had been inclement, and she wanted to be warm. She slipped on her winter boots.

Town Business

She drove a Dan-U Farm's truck, meaning a truck that advertised the cattle operation on the driver's door. Ruth took special pleasure in driving the farm's trucks into town. So many people had bet on her financial failure and her inability to stay in the business after her husband's death. For over two years, she received lowball offers from cattlemen who thought she might be fed up with the long hours and might be ready to sell the operation at any price. She was now a bona fide member of the Missouri Cattlemen's Association and was heartily greeted by Alcott County business owners. At least, that's the way it was as she remembered.

The county highway was long and hilly, the bare charcoal gray trees added to her sense that she was leaving the woodlands and going into the county's small commercial district. She pulled her truck into a diagonally marked parking space beside the court house. On the sidewalk, Ruth passed a World War I memorial, a soldier held an injured fellow. The elderly woman now vigorously climbed the granite steps and opened a massive oak door. The elevator wasn't far from the entry door, so she directed it to the third floor and the building department. She recognized the department's secretary as the night attendant at the hospital's elevated parking ramp; the hospital was regional, serving other counties.

"Can I help you?" the clerk said.

"I'm Ruth D. Uppers from Dan-U Farms. I applied for a building permit a month or so ago to build an addition to the farm's main house. My builder, Jim Schnelling said that there was some problem with that application. I like to know what the problem is and then cancel the project while I'm in town," Ruth said. The clerk shuffled through papers in a thick brown file, and then she went to a computer. She scrolled through files until she laughed aloud.

"Mrs. Uppers," the clerk said. "Nobody has signed this application. There's a note here. It looks to me like your builder came in one day and was going to sign the application, but his writing hand was heavily bandaged, and he wanted someone to just fill in his name, we couldn't do it," the clerk added. "You could probably fill out a new application as the owner and have the builder resubmit plans, then you could sign the form, and the builder would be able to start building soon." The clerk smiled as if she had found a solution for the older woman.

"The builder's hand was injured?" Ruth wanted the clerk to say more.

"It was bandaged; I'm surprised that he didn't let you in on his hand," the clerk said. "I knew your son, Mrs. Uppers. I knew Danny; he'd come over and listen to albums with my brother."

"You're a Whitehall, aren't you?" Ruth said. The clerk nodded. "One of these days, I'll make it over to your mom and dad's house. I remember the hayrack rides they put on in the fall," Ruth said. Those words made her feel old and out of touch. The rides were years ago.

"Daddy's passed on, but Mama would be happy to visit, not too many people come by," the clerk said.

"I'll take an application with me," Ruth said, embarrassed over not hearing of the father's death; she was also mentally scattered about the news of the builder's wounded hand. It was important not to exaggerate the news or to become fearful. She tried to remember if the Schnellings owned ATVs and if there was an easy access point between Dan-U Farms and their property. She thanked the clerk and went outside. She walked to her vehicle and saw a candy store; she'd take something sweet back to Hugh and buy herself a chocolate treat. She examined every bin, occasionally asking the counter help for a sample; she left with a full medium-sized bag. The wind was becoming brisk, but she decided to sit down on bench near the sidewalk. Ruth watched the cars go by and often identified the driver; a small town amusement. On the other side of the street was one of the town's two taverns.

Ruth was not surprised when Mike Galliwag left the establishment and moseyed down a cobblestone path. Sharleen Davis's car passed Galliwag twice, going up the street, and then turning around. She finally parked her Buick, and Ruth's former hired hand joined Davis in her automobile. After 15 minutes, Galliwag exited the vehicle and returned to the bar. Why wasn't Sharleen afraid of Galliwag? He was a rough-looking character by anyone's standards. Sharleen went into a beauty parlor; Ruth's hair was well-clipped, and she wasn't really ready for another haircut. Ruth entered the salon and acted as if she had happened into an uncanny meeting with Sharleen. "Well, you did make it safely through the night," Ruth told the widow. "I came to have my hair styled," Ruth laughed. Sharleen was obviously uncomfortable. Fortunately, Ruth's chair was beside the widow's seat, so they could talk.

"I once employed Mike Galliwag," Ruth said. "I saw you talking with him before you came in." the elderly woman added.

"Lord Mrs. Ruth, you're not following me, are you? I find it very coincidental to see you in town today." Sharleen examined her nails, noting a few chips in the enamel. "I need a redo on these two. She showed the beauty consultant the defective polish. She turned to Ruth. "I don't think you come into town to buy groceries; you send Connie Mae or David Paul," Sharleen said. "You want to know about Galliwag. When I was 16, I was married to Mike Galliwag for about three weeks. He gave me two black eyes during that time, and the marriage was annulled. No, nobody needs to tell me about him, Mrs. Ruth. Galliwag is the past that won't go away." Sharleen said.

"You let him into your car," Ruth said.

"What's your point, Mrs. Ruth? I don't care to be spied upon, don't care for it at all," Sharleen said.

"Sharleen honey," the salon owner said. "I'm sorry about your husband, unspeakable tragedy. I think one of his friends called here looking for you. Does the name Schnelling ring a bell,

Jim Schnelling? Yeah, I'm almost sure that was his name, he'd be Don's older boy wouldn't he, a contractor?" Sharleen nodded and glared at the woman as if the world were conspiring to reveal every one of her day's contacts with Ruth Uppers. "He'll call back, don't worry," said the woman. Ruth was silent; she saw no reason to be alarmed because Sharleen Davis and Jim Schnelling knew each other; everyone knew everyone in Alcott County.

The hairstylist wet her hair; that is, the lady wet half her hair; the wet side was pasted to her face. She watched the lazy activity at the tavern across the street through a dressed-up window. She abruptly turned her head; she stood and went to look through the glass with her smock still on. Ruth put her purse under her smock and fiddled with its contents. Ruth said, "Excuse me. I'll be back in a minute." Once outside, she watched Galliwag get into the passenger side of a Dan-U Farms' truck. Jim Schnelling was the driver. When the truck began to pull forward, Ruth aimed her pistol and shot a front tire twice, and then she shot the rear tire. She beeped Mix on her walkie-talkie, and told him to send "the men" to the main street. Schnelling ducked in the driver's seat, and Galliwag ran down the road, then between the buildings. Ruth approached the vehicle; she moved a tarp in the truck's bed.

She gasped. Jason Piny had been beaten so badly that he could only utter sounds to show his pain. People began to gather. "Somebody, call an ambulance," Ruth said. "Somebody get an ambulance," she repeated in a shaky voice. She sat on the curb, her hair in pins and gel.

About forty people assembled; the ambulance arrived, and the medics began to transport Jason from the truck bed to the emergency vehicle. Jim Schnelling had not moved from the driver's seat of the immobilized Dan-U Farms' truck. Sheriff Burns walked through the crowd; his squad car could be seen between bystanders. Ruth stood when it was clear he wanted to talk to her. Ruth explained, "I saw Jim Schnelling driving one of my trucks; Mike Galliwag joined him from the bar across the street. I fired shots to stop the car theft and found a Dan-U Farm's hired hand beaten in the back, Jason Piny. "He's hurt badly," Ruth said.

"You've a permit to carry a concealed weapon?" the sheriff asked. He left Ruth for a moment and chased off the local newspaper's photographer. The journalist snapped a picture of Schnelling in the stolen vehicle. He also caught the medics in action, working, repositioning the injured man as gently as possible. "Go on; go on, there's no news here. Go on home all of you," Clayborn Burns yelled to the crowd, then he returned to Ruth.

"That's Judge Alexander Jason Piny's son in the back of that truck," Ruth said with true knowledge of her employee's background. "He's a decorated veteran, and I insist that you hold Schnelling and Galliwag and whoever else figures into committing the crimes here," Ruth told the sheriff when he returned.

"Yeah, somebody better call the man's parents," Clayborn said. "Others saw the crime, I suppose." The lawman looked around and was mentally trying to identify the onlookers. The farm's Suburban parked; Mix, David Paul, Ray, and Lester, spotted Ruth and came to the elderly woman. Ruth was grateful that Wen had the good sense not to come on the scene. Ruth pointed to Jason, who was only now being moved inside the ambulance. Ray jumped inside the vehicle and would ride with his friend to the hospital. Lester reported that both of Jason's legs had been broken, and it was likely that the man was in shock.

"I don't want the Dan-U Farms' hands hanging around here. Send them back," the sheriff told Ruth. Ruth returned to the hair salon and looked for Sharleen Davis; quickly coming back to her group after the business's owner said that the woman went out the back door.

The deputy attempted to put handcuffs on Jim Schnelling, but the man showed the officer his wounded hand. Schnelling was directed to the backseat of the squad car. Sirens rang out, lights flashed. Ruth was going to tell Lester something; she opened her mouth, but the words failed, and she felt dizzy. She held onto Lester as if he would steady her. But David Paul lifted Ruth off her feet and carried the exhausted woman to her parked truck. He drove her home.

Days went by; Ruth was confined to her bed. The house seemed to be abandoned, with only David Paul who reported to Ruth's doctor, prepared her meals, and read newspapers to her in the quiet evening hours. Wen, Connie Mae, and Mix went to St. Louis when Connie Mae began having labor pains. Wen had called to check on Ruth's condition and also to relay Connie Mae's difficulties in giving birth to the twins. Connie Mae's doctors feared infections in the infants since the mother's water had broken far before the babies' births; twin girls. Of course, Jason Piny was on Ruth's mind. She asked David Paul for news, but on Ruth's doctor's orders, all information regarding the young man would be kept from her until she was stronger. David Paul brewed dark teas, and they sipped the herbal elixirs on a medicinal schedule. Ruth thought that he was an unlikely nurse, too young, boyish. Yet he took his nursing duties seriously and even screened phone calls. Ruth requested that her church's minister come to the house, so they might pray together, and she might be filled in on events at the church. David Paul protected her perfect rest and would not allow visitors for a while. Finally, Ruth heard a familiar car in the drive.

She pulled back the curtain and saw Connie Mae and her vehicle, but Wen wasn't with her. Ruth called David Paul and asked him to assist the young mother with her brood. In a few minutes, Connie Mae put down two infant girls on Ruth's bed. David Paul stayed with Hugh in the kitchen. Ruth gently stroked the girls' bald heads, Willa and Winona Wilson.

"Daddy is with Wen in St. Louis. While I was in the hospital, Wen visited the city's public library with a camera. They've arrested him, Mrs. Ruth. They've put him in jail, and I don't know if they're going to let him out." Connie Mae said. Ruth continued to caress the babies' heads. She lifted the newborns and tucked them in her blankets, and they were close to her own body. Ruth noted the shape of their eyes and the wetness of their saliva.

"Connie Mae, they're beautiful, the most delicate creatures I've ever seen," Ruth said.

"But Mrs. Ruth," Connie Mae said.

"Naw, naw, naw, shhhh," said Ruth. "I don't want you to fret about anything. We'll bring Wen home as soon as I can post his bond. They can't hold him very long for having a camera," Ruth concluded.

David Paul came into the room holding Hugh. "I think Mix and Wen just pulled into the lane," David Paul said. Connie Mae jumped up from her seat at Ruth's bedside and made her way outside. When Mix's truck stopped in the gravel parking spaces, Connie Mae ran to meet her husband. She held his hand and led him into the house. Mix followed behind the couple. The group congregated in Ruth's bedroom. Ruth wanted to hear all the news about the births and of Wen's arrest and eventual release. Mix puffed up his chest as if he had a story to tell. Connie Mae hugged Wen; she kissed him; there was no doubt that he belonged to her.

"Cost me a pretty bit of my savings to get this hooligan out of jail," Mix said. "Then the police moved Wen from jailhouse to jailhouse like a cat and mouse game. Spent nearly three days tracking him down and trying to find somebody to take the bail money," Mix added.

Wen held his hands out to Ruth as if he were offering her a gift. "My gorgeous girls," he said. The elderly woman smiled and viewed the infants' sleeping faces. She noted that Willa was sucking on her thumb. Mix pointed to himself as if he wanted some credit for the adorable girls. "Does my rescuer have a bottle of wine at the men's house for a little celebration?" Ruth advised Wen that wine was in the kitchen cupboard. In minutes, the celebrating father passed out glasses and uncorked the bottle. Mix's eyes shimmered for his granddaughters.

"Willa and Winona Wilson," said the grandfather. He tapped his glass against Wen's, then his daughter's, and then Ruth's. David Paul toasted but was in a hurry for the party to break up; only he knew the doctor's orders and had personally spoken with him. Ruth marveled at David Paul's serious demeanor and noted his anxiety about the commotion.

David Paul whispered to Connie Mae, and the mother suggested that she needed help in setting up the bassinettes. Wen assented, sensing now that many chores would call him away from idle comfort. The newborns fussed when they were awakened and moved into the nursery.

Mix held up his hand as if he wanted to make another declaration. David Paul nudged him from the room. "No more tonight, Mix," the young man said. "Mrs. Ruth is under strict orders."

"Mrs. Ruth is sick?" Mix asked. "That's a crying shame. Somebody ought to called me." Mix said. David Paul took the older hired hand by the arm and led him to the porch door. "Arrested Wen that's right, for carrying a camera on city property, whoever heard of such a thing?"

David Paul stopped. "Yes, strange," he said.

"Strange is the word for it. Who'd figure that my Connie Mae would marry somebody like Wen Wilson?"

"Are you all right?" David Paul asked Mix.

"Know the city like the back of my hand now. I've less money and new granddaughters. I'm okay," Mix said, as if the affirmative statement were the end of his excitement; Mix was resigned. Ruth heard the side door shut, and her eternally faithful hired hand was on the path to the men's house. David Paul was soon with her, and asked if she wanted him to read to her. She heard Wen already in the library and felt soothed by his attention to books and scholarship; she hoped that he was back to work, manipulating language so the nation might understand the challenge before it. She intently listened for noise, sounds of Wen working.

"No reading tonight," Ruth said, contented with the homey and only relative silence in the house, Hugh's small sentences and light voice, Connie Mae's evening ritual of using the bathroom sink." I'm strong enough now, well, you know David Paul honey, I cannot stay in bed forever. I'll miss the Christmas season, my baking, and my cakes; oh, I need to see Jason Piny. I must get up," Ruth said. "Tomorrow, you'll let me go, David Paul?" she said.

"Doctor says it's too early to go to town. I guess it wouldn't hurt if you walked around the farm," David Paul said. "Jason Piny's father has called several times, and I've told him that you're tired out and are unable to help him for the time being. Alexander Piny will call again," David Paul said, as if it were no matter, nothing to worry about one way or the other.

David kept her from group meals, so she would not be tempted to talk about heavy ideas with Wen. So in the morning, Ruth had her personal telephone directory brought to her room. Even before dressing, she contacted the earth-movers and confirmed their plans to re-store the runway; the men would arrive at Dan-U Farms after 10:30 AM today. She also telephoned Alexander Piny and reached only his answering service. She put on a pair of gray athletic sweat-pants, a buttoned-flannel blouse, and her work boots. Then Ruth told David Paul to saddle Lilly. She checked on the infants before she headed to-ward the barn.

Lilly, the old paint of the horses was as even as a deep forest board; the horse never went its own way but patiently awaited direction from Ruth's reins. Ruth speculated that Lilly had no genes for unruliness, and that her lineage might have led a general into battle; she was markedly obedient. The elderly farmwoman once again tucked her shiny pistol into a saddle pouch.

Lilly stirred long-plumed cock pheasants from their winter resting places in high tawny grass. Ruth directed the horse to the garage, where the airplane was kept, and then the woman rode up to the flat ridge, the place of the old runway; she awaited the bulldozers and hydraulic shovels. Ruth dismounted and let the horse loose. Lilly moved around in a small circle. Ruth found a seat atop the weeds and delighted in the chilly blue sky and its slight breeze. She thought about Mix and how he took his age and threw it about, only making himself look like an incompetent fool. Could he shake his low self-image and take charge in an emergency? Could he inwardly prompt the confidence to fly the plane out of the state, out of the country, if need be? Ruth looked down the grassy stretch and thought she noted a patch of colorful meadow flowers. She ignored the sight at first, so convinced that the bright sun and its glare were playing tricks on her increasingly feeble eyes. A gust of wind rolled across the ridge and where there were flowers, a resplendent white cloth took their place, characterless except as an outline and as an outline, it posed a man's peaceful figure. Ruth knelt on the rugged ground, mindful of smoothed stones half covered with topsoil. The breeze crossed her face, and a feeling of placidness came and overwhelmed her. She was surprised when large trucks carrying heavy equipment were beside her; she hadn't heard their roar or tussle on the hillside. A driver pulled up next to her, "Mrs. Uppers?" Ruth nodded. "We're going to make you leave the area while we're working," the operator said. "Could you tell that fellow down the field?" The man looked again. "He's left. I just saw him," the man said. Ruth found her horse and left the runway; she passed by the summer kitchen and then went back to the main house. Ruth tried again to reach Jason's father. She showered and dressed in her "church clothes;" it seemed that Ruth was going into town. She spoke of it to no one and then turned the key on her truck.

She inquired with the receptionist about the number of Jason Piny's room. She walked down a long corridor and finally came to a half circle desk in the middle of the floor. "I want to see Jason," Ruth told the nurse. The nurse wanted to know if she were a member of his family. Ruth truthfully shook her head, meaning no. The nurse advised Ruth that maybe the father would grant her permission; the nurse went on to say that Alexander J. Piny was in his son's room. The nurse would allow Ruth to pass with that understanding.

She hesitated and then went to talk to the older Mr. Piny. He was tall, broad-shouldered and had a full head of gray hair. "Judge Piny, I'm Ruth Uppers, and I'd like to see Jason if it's okay," the farmwoman said. Judge Piny was silent but extended his hand as if to give consent.

"He just stares off into space. Doctors say his body is healing, but I feel that I've lost my son," the old man said. Ruth approached Jason and gently massaged his eyes; it seemed that she was closing them for the first time in weeks. "I prayed for him.

I sit here, and I'm asking the Lord to bring him back from the shock of his injuries," the judge said. The son was in casts to his waist.

"Jason, the Lord is close to you, here with you now, and will answer prayers for you," the woman said. Judge Piny stood because he was teary-eyed and felt he might break down.

Ruth wiped away the old gentleman's tears with her finger. "Go home and rest," she told the father.

He smiled. "The motel room isn't home, and I keep thinking that if I stay here, he'll come around, some change in his expression, a couple of words." The judge's face once again contorted with pain, and his eyes were in pools of water, holding back, until drops rolled down his cheeks. Ruth put her arms around Jason's father, and he sobbed, leaning down on her shoulder.

"Judge, come to my house and stay the night. There're people, and, if only for the night, you can forget your troubles in conversations with others, a momentary rest from a huge burden," Ruth said. He turned backed to Jason, and Ruth knew that her invitation was a bust.

"Jason called you, Mrs. Ruth," the father said. "Mrs. Ruth, we need to talk, but today I'll be with him. Thank you for your support, so sympathetic.

I'm in no shape to be around strangers," said the older Piny. I just cannot leave him and must make arrangements to bring him closer to his family. He has brothers, many brothers, to look in on him," Piny said. Ruth watched Jason's facial movement; the muscles on the left twitched until his jaw dropped open. His head swung one way and then the other, and then Jason was very still. His dark penny eyes seemed to follow his father's two-tone watchband. His mouth opened.

"Father, what time is it?" Jason said.

The father was silent; he stooped to his knees, tears streaming down his face. "Jason, it's 2:00 P.M.," Judge Piny replied. The father then stood and brought his son's head close to him, messing his hair, surrounding his son's face with large hands. "The time is that of the Lord's powerful grace," the man added. "I've seen mercy," the older Piny cried and sat down in his former seat. Judge Piny folded his hands together as if he sat in prayer and meditation. Ruth and Judge Piny ordered supper trays from the hospital cafeteria; the farmwoman was out past her own doctor's orders, and so beeped David Paul and reported her whereabouts. Before long, Lester Grimes was at the nurses' station, waiting to escort Ruth home.

Ruth told the judge about her waiting hired hand and reissued an invitation to the farm.

"Yes, we must talk. You're the one who kindly offers refuge to Wendell Wilson. He's tragically intelligent. I was one of the first to see how Wen recognized the pattern in the puzzle," said Judge Piny. I saw the progression in his logic and knew it wouldn't be too long before he put it together." Ruth's face registered fear; she imagined that Alexander Piny was with the Culture Bureau, and that she was duped by his gentle mannerisms and sorrow.

"The judge is okay," Jason told Ruth. Judge Piny smiled, tears once again flowing down his face. The farmwoman opened her purse and gave the grateful father tissues. The move revealed her silver pistol. The judge pretended not to see the gun, and still, felt an urge to comment about the weapon.

"I think in the wild West the day always came when the gunslinger met his match," the judge said.

"I, sir, am neither outlaw nor gangster. I first shot soup cans with my brother, a man who was killed in WWII." Ruth turned to Jason. "I'll be back as soon as David Paul gives me permission." Ruth laughed aloud at the thought of a young man giving her limits. "It was a pleasure to meet you, Judge Piny, and do come to the farm. The judge nodded and said that they would talk more. Ruth followed the blue carpeted hallway to Lester; he leaned against the counter of the nurse's desk and read a sports magazine, quickly returning it to the stack. Once at Dan-U Farms, Lester went to the men's house, and David Paul put his wayward employer to bed.

Ruth felt increasingly strong as the days went by, and told David Paul to find a Christmas tree from the hillside pines. The effort soon inspired all the household members, and Ruth heard living room furniture being moved to make space for the hearty tree. Ruth told Connie Mae about a box of ornaments and lights underneath the blanket shelf in the linen closet. Hugh played with the figures from the nativity scene; the young boy mimicked an earthy farm conversation about moving herds and placing bulls. Colored-glass balls lined the tree's fresh branches, and blinking lights added to their attractiveness. Church members sent chocolates, oranges, and apples, fulfilling their annual ritual. Today, of all things, Ruth had it in her mind to make pizza; in the afternoon she fussed with the crusts' dough. The phone rang. Connie Mae answered the telephone, and it was the old judge, who told of his intentions to visit the farm before Jason was sent home to be cared for by in-home nursing and his brothers. Connie Mae gave Ruth the receiver, and the date was set for the evening. Ruth delighted in the father's visit and was interested in Jason's well-being.

Lester Grimes led the older Piny to the main house. When the escort was complete, the hired hand retreated to the men's house. No outsider was allowed to come on the farm without security guides. Alexander Piny entered the kitchen's foyer with grocery bags; the bags were filled with grated cheeses, green and red peppers, tomato sauce, and a jar of mushrooms. He put the sacks on the counter, emptied their contents; then he found an apron hanging from the refrigerator door's handle. He put it on, signaling that he was set for action. Hugh clung to Ruth's leg from the towering sight of the lanky stranger. Pizza it was; the two joined forced, throwing dough, chopping peppers, and spreading the many ingredients onto pans. Piny took a candy caramel from the pocket of his khaki trousers and gave it to Hugh; the child showed the treasure to his parents, and Wen Wilson came from the library into the kitchen. "I understand that you read John Milton," the judge said to Wen.

"Alexander Piny?" Wen said. The judge nodded. "I read mostly Areopagitica," Wen said. Wen held out his hand to the older Piny and zestfully greeted the judge. "Thank you for everything," Wen said.

"I'm glad to finally meet you, Wen. It's an honor to be in your company. I've admired your wits for a long time," the judge said, offering a warm smile to the writer. "I know many people whose help is for the asking," the judge added. Connie Mae entered the room, eyeing the seemingly pleasant visitor. The wife was sure that there was something odd about the judge's initial exchange. She supposed that John Milton was a current political thinker, but she had never heard of him, had never seen her husband with a work by the author.

"I'm sorry about your son, am glad he's doing better. I like Jason, he's as polite as they come around a cattle farm," said Connie Mae. Wen approved of Connie's praise for the hired hand, smiling at her words. The judge's expression was both light and deep with appreciation. Ruth supposed that his son's healthful rebound freed the man from grief: the judge was hopeful again.

"Thank you," the judge said spiritedly.

"You're my husband's patron, aren't you?" Connie Mae said as she looked at Wen and his easy sense of familiarity with Piny. Ruth knew that Connie Mae did not like the idea of being left out of her husband's dealings. The newborn infants cried like a choir in the back bedroom. Connie Mae looked at the judge, and left before Piny could respond to the inquiry. The judge gestured to Wen about his wonderment: how did she know? His arms went up briefly and signaled surprise over the wife's intuition. Ruth waited for the writer to respond.

"She's okay," Wen told the judge, indicating that her knowledge about Piny's authentic identity posed no problem. "Judge Piny, I'm also very sorry about Jason. I suppose the attack against him shows that the culture agents are aware of your patronage and position in the movement." Wen knew that he was informing Ruth of the judge's special ties to a resistance effort.

Wen's forthright statement took the judge back; he seemed not yet ready for openness. "I think the oven is probably hot enough for the pizzas," said Piny. Ruth felt odd excitement about the possibility of others who recognized Wen's powers of analysis and his ability to surmise public structures. She handed Judge Piny potholders, and it was as if they were a team. Ruth observed the judge throughout dinner; she felt especially close to Jason's old dad. His complexion was dark, almost too tanned for winter. His facial features looked as if fine light wood had come to life, there was an almost perfection in the detail, a strongly made nose and red raspberry lips, not thick, not thin. He looked ethical to Ruth, if such an appearance was possible. After dinner, Piny escorted Ruth to the screened side porch; she briefly pretended that the man was an eloquent suitor, and that youth was a factor in their lives.

Alex Piny

⤳

The moonlight shimmered on a parked car's chrome. The judge moved close to her on a rattan couch. He cleared his throat and seemed hesitant to start the necessary words. "I'm Wen Wilson's financial sponsor." The judge coughed again in the night air. "Mrs. Ruth, I recognized his unusual brightness many years ago after reading a short pamphlet on basic rights. His insights are impeccable; his articulation is unsurpassed," the judge said. "The changes began, and his words became more and more prophetic. He has a handle on what is going on." Midget and Harry whined outside the screened area; it was rare for them to be out. The dogs scratched against the entrance's door. Ruth could faintly hear newborns crying inside.

"Jason?" Ruth asked.

"Jason volunteered to guard over Wen when we found out where he was. He was happy to bring his stallion to a farm," the judge clasped his hands together. "His mother was the real equestrian in the family; she loved the animals and passed the fondness on." The man was silent. The two sat in silence for a long while. Then finally Ruth stood and let Midget and Harry in. "She's been gone for six years now." The dogs settled in the corner. "When I talk about her, it doesn't seem possible; death is an incredible thing when it comes to a spouse," the judge said. Ruth could have argued about degrees of tragedy, about impacts and disbelief, but she let the topic drop. It was not her place to put perverse blue ribbons on sorrowful events. Mix and David Paul opened the house door and stood for a moment to say goodnight.

"You shouldn't stay out. Doctor's orders," said David Paul. Mix assessed the judge from his role as the elder male on the farm. His hands were deep in his overall pockets, and he was notably focused on the old Piny. Ruth waved her hand at David Paul, who was being more of a caretaker than she expected from a cattle hire. David smiled and nudged Ruth a bit.

"Oh go on, you two," Ruth said in protest. The exiting men chuckled and made their way to the men's house. She could hear their voices rise as the men climbed the hill. "I'm ready to go in," Ruth said to the visiting gentleman. Judge Piny moved Ruth's face to him and gently kissed her on the lips. Ruth immediately stood, as if she were going inside. He gently pulled her back to her seat. "I'm an old woman. I don't appreciate your overture," she said. He caressed her hand; she brought it back to her side. "I know about you Pinys," Ruth said. She stood again like she were going in but did not move. As if another being, she led the judge into the unlighted house. Only a small nightlight shone in the hallway to her bedroom. Ruth walked to her room, and the judge followed. She pulled the window shades and turned on the light in the connecting bathroom. She shut the door and sat on a made bed.

"I'm an old man," said the judge as he untied and removed his shoes. He went into the bathroom and returned naked, like a willowy tree. Ruth pulled down the bedding so he could find his place and cover himself. Ruth undressed and put on a cotton nightgown. She tried to stay awake so that she could savor the warmth of his body, the beating of his heart, and the scent of men's deodorant on her sheets. One large arm kept her close to his figure. In the middle of the night, he awakened her. She agreed: he should not stay until morning. Before he left, the judge sat on the bedside. "I want to move Wen and family as soon as possible." Ruth turned to see the clock. "I'm going to make arrangements for my son, am sending him home." Ruth nodded. The judge slipped out of the bedroom, out the kitchen, and out of the house. She listened to the sound of his automobile. She wondered about their encounter, and then pushed thoughts about it from her mind. She wouldn't act like a schoolgirl at her age.

When the businesses opened, about 9:00 AM, she sold Dan-U Farm's last herd. Wen and Connie Mae overheard the transaction on account of the main house having one telephone. Ruth waited for questions about her dealings, but the couple seemed to know that a move was imminent. Hugh rested on the floor near a heat duct; he was chilled from an ear infection fever. The twins seemed to fuss in turns, one cried and then the other. Ruth put on a red plaid wool coat and fancy leather hat. "I'm going out," she said.

Ice was on the road in patches, and the leafless trees were dense and upright like straws on a broom. Ruth maneuvered her Suburban around the sharp, nearly hairpin turns of the road into town. She felt the newly bought concealed holster grip her shoulders. She was unrepentant about carrying the pistol since Jason's attack. She momentarily grieved that she no longer trusted the locals. But she didn't; she imagined that financially struggling people were more hoodwinked with cash rewards. She was thinking of Galliwag, was he bought or simply hateful? A wrench was cast into her human nature theories in the case of Jim Schnelling: he was neither poor nor notably unpleasant, and he had trespassed on her property with an ATV, threatening Jason first. Sharleen Davis was the grand riddle. Ruth sighed at the duplicity of her former attorney's wife. Reverend Phil was the great let down. The recount of characters stopped when she pulled into the church's parking lot. She turned the vehicle off and walked on the paving stones to the church office. It was an initial meeting for the cattlewoman and the interim minister. Reverend Phil left in the midst of commotion. She opened the solid exterior door and followed worn carpets to meet Trevor Roy.

She knocked on a painted door, "Reverend Roy?" she said. A short slender man answered the call, looking inquisitive. He extended his hand for an introduction. "I'm Ruth Uppers, a longtime member of First Presbyterian." The reverend shook her hand and proceeded to go behind his desk. His dark eyes almost crossed as an expression of gravity, he gave a short smile. "Wen Wilson called you about the possibility of having the infants baptized at a regular service. I told him I'd stop in and discuss the details, what you have in mind," Ruth said.

"I-I-I-I…am in favor of a private ceremony, at the altar," said Reverend Roy. The minister caught a glimpse of Ruth's holster strap. He looked, then hesitated, and began speaking, "Mrs. Uppers, do you plan to shoot me?" he asked. Ruth was embarrassed and pulled her coat together.

"Oh heavens, no," she quickly retorted. The minister smiled and became serious again.

"I'm just back from talking to Michael Galliwag over at the jail. I'm familiar with Jason Piny and the charges filed against him this morning. Of course, Galliwag contends that he was vigilante justice, and Piny's beating was on account of the sexual assault against Mrs. Davis."

"Sexual assault?" Ruth said.

"First degree, rape," the minister clarified his visitor's apparent misunderstanding. "If you want to remove the gun, we can go into the sanctuary, and I'll do a quick go-over of the ceremony," Reverend Roy said. Ruth took off her coat and unfastened the harness, putting the weapon on the clergy's desk. He opened a side drawer and was about to store the gun when Ruth asked about the drawer's contents; a Bible, Reverend Phil's Bible was on top of papers.

"I'll send Phil's Bible to his new address. I'm sure he'd want it." Ruth was startled to see the book left behind. Reverend Roy handed the Bible to Ruth. Ruth opened the cover and saw the handwritten words: To Philip, Love Mother, Christmas, 1992. She trembled over the abandoned item. "Yes," she said pulling herself together. "Tell me more about Piny's trouble," she stood, with the Bible in her hand and made way to the sanctuary. Roy spoke behind her.

"His father is expected to request a venue change with Jason's close association with the Wilson man," the reverend said. Townspeople say you've been more than warned about Wen Wilson, and you still won't put him out. Speculation is that Jason Piny was a hired bodyguard for the agitator." Reverend Roy played with a doorstop at the chapel's entry.

"Now, Mrs. Uppers, I don't know you at all. But people say you're a respected woman in the county."

"Don't believe people," Ruth said tersely.

"You're not a respected woman then?" the reverend said. It surprised her that he seemed ready for a confession.

Ruth might have unconsciously rolled her eyes at the questioner. "I sir, am the owner of a cattle farm. I try to be generous to the community. I try to mind my own business; now I have a mind to defend my household members from anyone who maliciously comes on my land."

The minister seemed to search the heavens for an advance answer with his eyes, looking upward. "Why would anyone come onto your land with malice?" The reverend thought he had closed the cross-examination. The rattling of locks could be heard near the office.

Ruth stretched her head around the corner, seeing the victimized Sharleen Davis. Ruth raised her eyebrows. Reverend Roy whispered, "She's here for spiritual counseling." He quickly went through the pre-worship service baptisms, and Ruth now followed him back to the lobby. Ruth stood silently beside Jason's accuser. The minister retrieved Ruth's gun from his desk drawer. Ruth strapped the thick brown leather holster over her shoulders, and the woman gasped.

Sharleen began weeping, her eye make-up rolling down her cheeks having an appearance of soot. "Woman, you've gone mad, carrying firearms around town." Sharleen reached in her purse for a tissue. "You've hired shady men to protect Wen Wilson. Well, Paul knew Wen Wilson was

nobody, an intellectual sham, no genius, no benefit to anyone, not in his book."

"Sharleen, you invited Jason to your home.
I've witnesses," Ruth said. Sharleen howled and
held on to the minister's arm so she wouldn't collapse. Reverend Roy shook his head in disapproval.

"Go, Mrs. Uppers. Go. This woman has been
traumatized by the death of a dear husband as
well as the fellow's crime," the minister said. Ruth
pushed back against the man's nudge and tried to
make eye contact with Sharleen. Ruth was certain
that the woman couldn't lie if there was a direct
confrontation.

"Jason told me about going to your house
shortly after Paul passed away." Ruth said, as the
minister grew more forceful with her, moving her
to the exterior door. Ruth held up Reverend Phil's
Bible. "Reverend Phil wouldn't have left without
this, a Christmas gift from his mother." Reverend
Roy now held her firmly by the arm. His eyes were
black, like bite-sized licorice. Saliva was near his
lips as if he might spit his words, his rebuke.

"Have you lost your sense, Mrs. Uppers?"
Ruth thought he might put his hands on his
hips, emphasizing his impatient disgust. His
head bobbed forward and back as he spoke of his

sympathy for Sharleen Davis. "Let's be compassionate with the broken-hearted," he told Ruth.

"There is a young man in this county's hospital that has two broken legs. I'm not for "free love," and Sharleen's and Jason's association so soon after her husband's death is a mystery to me, but good Reverend Roy, that man is no rapist and that woman is not the victim she claims," Ruth said with conviction, causing the minister to shake his head in disagreement. She clutched Phil Boxer's Bible next to her bosom. "Phil would not have left this Bible," she said.

"Your point?" Reverend Roy said. Ruth was silent, sliding her boot across the gravel.

"Go home, Mrs. Uppers. I've an appointment now but will have someone familiar with your circumstances look in on you. Okay?" Ruth nodded, feeling the keenest betrayal from the churchman. She went to her truck and took a brimmed brown hat from the cab. She adjusted it on her head. Ruth decided to walk to the town square; the cattlewoman was feeling alone, and her gait was sad. Perhaps her credibility slipped with age: older women lacked authority. She chuckled to herself as she imagined a hard reality. People might write lists and review chores while conversing with her. She sat on a green painted park bench.

Gray and white pigeons flocked around a discarded fast-food bag, picking out a wrapped bun. There were too many birds for any one bird to have a satisfying lunch. Still, they skittered like a bi-colored piece of sod. One pigeon remained apart from the crowd. Blue spots dotted its white feathers on account of its playful interest in a broken ink pen. The bird flipped the pen over its back, carried it in its beak like an expensive cigar. The bird scratched at the pen when it fell on the ground. It seemed unaware of the scramble for the bread.

Ruth watched the downtown shoppers and marveled at the idea of a brave entrepreneur opening a candle store with candles being an only inventory. She saw the clothing store and wondered about when the last dress was sold in the unfashionable former warehouse.

Ruth saw Clayborn Burns pull his squad car to the curb. He opened the car's door, began walking across the bristly pale grass. He stopped in front of Ruth's bench and acted as if he were assessing the park, slowly looking over her head, from North to South. He finally took off his hat and sat down beside her. "Jim's wife bailed him out; Sharleen Davis paid Galliwag's," the sheriff said. The sheriff glanced over to her, noting her reactions. "I'm going to call your nephew Billy Buzzy and see if he can't hire professional care for you," he said.

The birds meandered to the bandstand. Ruth visually followed their path from bits of the torn hamburger sack. "There was a white pigeon that had colored itself from playing with an old broken ink pen." Ruth moved her head, trying to find it. "I don't see it now," she said. "Anyway, it had blue polka dots." The sheriff smiled in only a mannerly way. "I can't believe your words; I mean Billy Buzzy hasn't been in Missouri since he discovered showgirls."

"He'll come back to take care of Dan-U Farms' business, its money for auntie," the blunt sheriff said. "You can think of me whatever you want. The way I figure, you're a stubborn and stupid woman and while you're probably not senile, you've stirred up enough trouble in this county that nobody cares," he said. He laughed. "The Presbyterian minister called me and warned me that you were carrying a gun. I roared after I put down the phone. See, he no longer knows that you're the proper Mrs. Uppers, and if you're walking around with a gun, then the world's gone bad. Frankly, people don't understand the company you now keep," the sheriff said. He looked at Reverend Phil's Bible on her lap, "I've seen it all, a Good Book and a gun." The sheriff put on his hat and was ready to stand, was happy with his scolding.

"The gun stays; the Bible belongs to Reverend Phil. I'm going to call his new place to see about sending it to him." She now looked at the sheriff. "You see, it was a Christmas gift from his mother in celebration of his ordination," Ruth said. She opened the book; an airline ticket fell from its pages. Ruth trembled when she picked it up. It wasn't used and was valid. "Sheriff, I'll go with you to the courthouse and fill a missing persons' report," Ruth said.

"No, Mrs. Ruth I can't let you do that," the sheriff said, as he held put his hand for Phil's Bible. Ruth pulled back while staring him in the eyes; she accused him of having insider knowledge of the oddities and yet never said a word. Gipsy pigeons clucked overhead, an erratic commotion and were like conjoined shadows against a crisply clear winter sky. "I warned you from the start," he said. Ruth watched her adversary walk across the field to his car.

On her way home, the cattlewoman realized that she accomplished nothing, had called a negative attention to herself. She wasn't a sleuth or a television detective. Unused flight tickets didn't necessarily signal wrong-doing. Reverend Roy was convinced that she was senile. She threw her brimmed suede hat on the passenger's seat and smiled. Of course, the Reverend wasn't familiar with women farmers, and she probably looked like a rough hobo. She was driving parallel to the farm's fence line on a long straightaway when Ruth saw an eerie red reflection on the bare trees; a car was in the ditch. She slowed down and took off her coat so she could quickly access her pistol. She removed a plastic flashlight from the glove box. From inside the cab, she swept the scene with her light. The car door opened, and in twilight, Ruth could see Alexander Piny, his figure was over the partially buried vehicle, and he was stepping onto the pavement, approaching the familiar pick-up. She put down the window. Piny was unhurt, mostly embarrassed to be helpless and in the brush.

"They're out," Piny said. Ruth nodded, indicating that she knew bail was posted for both men.

"You almost made it to the gate," Ruth said, while motioning the judge into her truck. A smiled was exchanged between them before the judge left the window and sat beside her in the cab. "Don't ask me how I know, the day seems like a lengthy story, but I'm very sorry about the charge against Jason," Ruth said. "I'm overwhelmed with injustice." Piny audibly winced from a cut that ran across one hand's fingers. "A cloth is in the box," she said. At the farm's lane, she punched in her electronic code to open high security gates. She drove slowly and could hear the over-sized gravel popping under the truck's tires: it was a day!

The kitchen was busy and festive, smelling at once of fried chicken and apple-cinnamon cake. Connie Mae and David Paul were in matching aprons; Ruth had gone to a sale and a single apron pattern was available, featuring printed green sprigs and the herb's name in fancy lettering. Ray Caro and Lester Grimes sat on the couch in the living room, playing guitars. Hugh stacked red, blue, and yellow blocks in front of the men, and then knocked them over and shrieked with joy when he saw the elderly woman and her friend. She took down a large salad bowl and filled it with warm sudsy water. Ruth cleaned Piny's injury, and then she brought out a plain crystal decanter filled with expensive bourbon. She liked bourbon. She hung up the coats and hats before she took down the whiskey tumblers; she was wearing her holster. Yet, the group was perceptive, knowing exactly when not to bug Ruth.

"Trouble in town?" Connie Mae said diffidently, as she put full plates before the arrivals.

Ruth ignored her question when Wen moseyed into the room. He needed a pencil and put Connie Mae and David Paul in motion from his request. His wire rims were lost; he wore heavy black-framed eyeglasses. In her testy mood, she thought he looked like a replica of Buddy Holly.

"Mix is with the girls," Wen told her, not seeming to notice the judge's cut hand or her gun and holster. Ruth poured another shot and drank it. She could feel rising irritation at his self-absorption.

"You want a pencil?" Ruth opened. "Who're you that you can't see people are being hurt around you, missing, beaten, falsely charged, and run off roads," Ruth said. Piny shook his head at Ruth's outburst, thinking it counterproductive at the moment. "Today, I'd give nothing for your musings. It's time to go, Wen Wilson." Ruth began to cry; Piny waved the scholar away. David Paul followed Wen as far as the living room and sat out Ruth's storm.

"Eat, Ruth," said the protective judge. "I bet you've been in town all day and didn't stop for a bite. You don't need any more of this," he said, as he took the decanter off the table.

"We've things to discuss, serious things, and I don't want you soused. I haven't had fried chicken in a long while." The judge placed a napkin on his lap. "Thank you, Connie Mae; it was good of you to think of us." Ray and Lester packed up their guitars, politely saying goodbye. Wen backed his way from the table, and then quickly returned to the library. He was upset. "Ruth, I'm going to move Wen and his family to Bern, Switzerland; the papers are being processed," Piny said. "I'm going to care for everyone on the farm, the kids, the guitar pickers, David Paul, and Mix. I want you to join me as my wife." Piny dipped the injured hand into the water. Connie Mae moved closer toward the two, putting dishtowels away.

"Your wife?" Ruth said with amusement. "Oh dear, Judge Piny, I've had a stressful day."

Ruth pushed the bones to the side of her plate and concentrated on the mashed potatoes. Connie Mae put a slice of dessert above their dinner plates; they nodded in appreciation.

Ruth began to suspect that the judge was sincere; he was asking her to marry him. Might he still be in a state of shock from the accident? She cleared her own dishes. Ruth put on coffee. "I'm rightly flattered Alex; I can call you Alex since you've asked me to be your wife. But are you sure you're not suffering from a head injury?" she said. He smiled fully at the farm woman.

"I knew the day Jason's mind came back, and he spoke," Piny said, with tears welling in his eyes. "Your prayers raised two men from the dead; he was lost to me, and you gave me hope." Ruth poured crème into her cup of coffee. She seemed too somber for the judge's expressed words.

"Jason's in trouble," Ruth said.

"I can work with that kind of trouble," Piny said. Ruth thought Alex cried more often than she was used to in a man; his tears mildly shocked her system and yet somehow she believed in his masculine uprightness, meaning she sensed honor in his public and private dealings. She felt kinship with him in that quality; she felt extraordinary empathy for him as a grieving father. Ruth caught Connie Mae gripped in the romantic drama, staring at a newly-revealed couple and leaning against the kitchen cabinet in a dumbstruck pose. The older women shooed her on. Connie Mae exited the room, sliding on her socks like a girl.

"I'm alone and you're alone. I suppose that we happily could stay that way, but I believe we're a pair. Marry me," he said. Ruth already decided in his favor, but felt she couldn't be too easy.

She stood and removed her gun harness. "All I know about you is that you're a financial patron of an agitator," Ruth said. "They call you 'judge,' so I guess you've sat at a bench. I'll marry you and suspend caution for discovery," Ruth said. He smiled, remaining quiet and thoughtful. She sounded hard in her own mind. "We can make a life together. We'll overcome difficulties." Mix and David Paul came from the nursery and were off to the men's house.

Mix stopped in front of the judge and gave him an exaggerated glare. "You want to step outside?" the old hired hand said. The judge smiled but wasn't sure of what to do with the humor. Mix slapped his knee and laughed and laughed. He loved teasing suitors; it was a Missouri tradition. The judge stood, tenderly folding his arms around his fiancé, but Piny was interrupted when the writer entered the kitchen. He held out his hand to the old judge to signal congratulations. The news spread as quickly as the infants' cries. Ruth, peeved at Wen, drew bathwater. She hung her holster in her room. She returned to the room with a blanket and pillow. Alex took them from her and looked over at the couch; he winked at her.

She smiled and said, "Wen, we'll talk tomorrow." She pointed to the Christmas lights and asked the judge to unplug them; only two days before Christmas, and she was as tired as a secondhand doll. She went to her bath and closed the door. Oddly, she had agreed to be Alex's wife, and at the moment, she longed for privacy, for somewhere to sort out recent events. She looked at her pale and freckled skin and shut her eyes. The elderly were also entitled to intimate companionship. Ruth felt a physical flutter when she looked at Alex's figure. Her silliness needed to stop; nobody in the world was allowed to be "in love" with so many pressing responsibilities. The Lord designated Wen to be a genius; she believed it was a handicap, a mental flaw, at times. What good were the best words if they were so misjudged?

She dried herself and put on her nightgown. She took a last look at her pistol and holster and went to bed. Half asleep, she dreamed voices, boisterous collaborations, and tires rolling upon loose rock. She heard tenors, young men's proclamations about an uneasy effort. Alex was standing at her door in the morning; he was in a hurry to travel to the next county's courthouse. He sat at the end of her bed and watched as she pulled out a navy blue suit from the closet. Alex frowned.

He stood and went through her wardrobe of dress clothes. He held up a rose-colored suit, and Ruth put it on in his presence. Alex was pleased.

"Leave the gun," he said. "You're about to become the wife of a court's officer. I don't do weapons," he whispered so not to wake the rest of the house members. Ruth took Alex's words as a command.

"If you want a wife, sir, I'll be it. I'll not be your child in need of a keeper," she replied.

He nodded, realizing her spirit, a spirit he intended to refine more after they left the daily intrigue of Wen's adversaries. Ruth was sure he was no hayseed and would demand more sophistication from a partner. He put his overcoat on and suggested that he would drive to the Justice of the Peace. A heavy snow began to fall after they pulled onto the highway; it was a slow and cautious drive on the curvy iced roads, but finally they arrived before the nineteenth century building. Alex stopped the Suburban and came around to open Ruth's door.

"I'll want to spoil you," he said.

"I'm much too practical to ever be spoiled," she said, catching a snowflake on her lip. He smiled as if her words assured him he had made the right decision in asking her to marry him.

The civil marriage ceremony, with the paper-work, took about an hour. On the way from the courthouse, the couple passed a bronze soldier memorial from WWI. Snow filled the crack and crevices of the human look-alikes. An image of her son came into her mind; it was quickly pushed back in her many thoughts. Her mind was as if a receptacle for disquieting memories, perhaps the last passing of repressed sorrows and the awakening of another life. She turned back to the icy doughboys; the past, the tagalong past had been a weight for too long. "Do you want to stop for coffee or tea at one of these shops?" Alex said.

"Yes," she said. They walked to a downtown diner and split a stack of pancakes. Ruth diluted her coffee with crème. "Have you talked to Wen about moving to Switzerland? We discussed a move only to Canada," she sighed. "You've changed our plans."

'Why, you're just married, and you want to talk about your boarders?" Alex teased her, as if wanting the first hours of their marriage to be light and carefree. "I won't have the new Mrs. Piny frazzling about the tasks ahead. My dear, you need greater faith and still more courage…without the weapon," he said. Ruth detected a bit of bossiness in her husband and thought she better end it from the onset. She sipped her coffee, aware of noise, plates colliding. She would handle Alex's bossiness later. She couldn't believe it. Clayborn Burns, Mike Galliwag, and Sharleen Davis were being seated at a table at the front.

Ruth pointed at the odd trio with her spoon. Alex turned, and then quickly turned back. "The neighboring counties are popular," Ruth smiled but was unsure about the chance meeting. Ruth changed the subject. "Wen needs you to guide him, and we both know he must go."

"Who is the man in the middle?"

"That's Mike Galliwag, the one that beat Jason. The cops and the robbers are having a social," Ruth announced. Alex face seemed to go blank as a result of his thought. He stood and aggressively began his way to the brutal diner. Ruth followed after him, was determined to stop a confrontation. The trio was surprised at the tall man's anger; they had never seen him, but they immediately recognized Ruth. Sharleen stood and poked a finger in the air.

"Arrest her, Clayborn! She's following me. She's following me." Sharleen's voice began to give in her distress. "Don't you understand, she's following me," Sharleen wailed, full of tears. Ruth stepped closer to her, and Sharleen collapsed onto her bosom. Ruth tried to comfort the nervous woman.

Galliwag smirked, showing a glint from gold-filling. "Who are you?" Galliwag spoke to Alex.

"I'm Jason Piny's father," the judge said. Galliwag chuckled. Alex seemed to debate whether to pull Galliwag from his chair. His temple vein throbbed as he looked at the ruffian. The sheriff stood, sensing trouble.

"What do you want?" the sheriff said. He led Alex to the door. "I'll get your tab, Judge Piny. You and Mrs. Uppers head on back to Dan-U Farms," he said. Ruth showed him her wedding ring. "Oh Lord, don't tell me that Judge Alexander Piny and Mrs. Ruth are married. Lord, Lord, the world's got problems now. I want you both to head on back," Sheriff Burns said.

"Piny," Galliwag said. "I stuffed Jason's balls in his asshole. Maybe you should look," Alex leaped backwards onto the breakfast table and dishes crashed to the floor. Alex held Galliwag's nose in an upright family-sized bowl of sausage gravy. Sharleen screamed and fell to her knees. The sheriff called for backups, pulling Piny from the drowning man.

"Go just, go," the owner pleaded. Alex stood; jelly was on his face. Ruth pushed Alex out the door.

"Well, Alex, don't talk to me anymore about civil ways. "You've trashed a local café with your good manners," Ruth said. She plucked the flower from her lapel and went to the driver's side of the Suburban. She offered no options; she was driving. Ruth reached into the vehicle's center console and removed saved napkins so that Alex could wipe his face.

"I've wanted to run into that guy," Alex said with excitement. The scuffle energized the older man. The trip back to the farm was quiet, with both newlyweds contemplative from the morning's events. Once inside the house, Ruth retired to her, their, bedroom and put on everyday clothes. David Paul brought in Jason's extra work jeans for oversized Alex.

Ruth intended to show her new husband the farm and supposed that they'd ride horses to the pastures. She was practical, and through her practicality, she hoped to consummate a marriage. She rummaged in drawers for land maps and boundaries lines. She would also show yearly financial and tax records. Alex, she noted, hesitated to leave the bedroom; he had other plans. She pulled the window blinds and rested beside Alex's change of pants. Alex stripped to a bare nothing, not quite gray body hair, thin legs, and of course, he was ready for love. Ruth would have preferred to go over the details of farming operation, but no good.

Old women stop imagining physical love, and now Alex was performing like a younger man. She listened to his breath as he climaxed, and she was satisfied with the interaction.

Afterwards, she tried to dress, and he slightly pulled on her arm as if he wanted her to do it again later. So she stayed, unaccustomed to the two "selves" and considerations of new wedlock. Finally, he was tired. Ruth dressed and sat on the bedside; she decided to go into the fields. She passed Wen on her way out; he was holding Willa and she cried from an infected ear.

"Courier dropped off an envelope," Wen pointed to its resting spot on the counter. Ruth nodded and tore the packages' seal. She removed travel plans, several tickets to Bern; she firmly held them, feeling emotions sink at the thought of leaving Dan-U Farms. The baby's face was red, and the father tried to soothe the infant. He walked to a bedroom in an effort to give Ruth quiet. Ruth returned to the long-awaited papers and exited the kitchen. Her eyes followed her boot tips past the men's house, past the stable, and up to a path that led to highlands. Of course, she would leave; she was married and obligated to go with Alex. Bern? Europe? She wasn't an internationalist; she was elderly. Willa's tears had to be contagious.

She wiped her eyes and stepped-up her walking pace. Her memories were in Missouri. Ruth reached the hill's peak and the newly constructed runway. Mix worked on the twin engine; it had been moved for a quick getaway. The past months seemed so unlikely to her, the marriage, the many incredible players, and now the prospect of going abroad. She watched Mix turn a large wrench at one of the plane's engine. Suddenly, Ruth noted Wen who had followed her from the house; he was out of breath from a hurried pace. She looked at him in a questioning way, as if wondering why he needed to speak with her and why he hadn't let her go alone. She wanted to be alone with her thoughts.

"The judge told us to start packing," he said. Ruth nodded. The time had come for a new circumstance, still she imagined little different might come from the move. She had many unanswered questions.

"It's time," Ruth said in a tired voice. She watched Mix fire up the plane's engines. She had told Wen the answer she wanted herself. Yes, it was time, for better or for worse; it was time for fresh scenes. Deep down, she thought herself too old for a happier life in a foreign country, but she had prepared for the move; the cattle were sold, the hired hands were looking for other jobs. And she was a married woman, which made a decision only part hers. "You know, I came up here so I could blame you in private. Our friendship has cost much," she said.

"I know," Wen said. "You've been distant with me lately. I knew you were adding up the cost."

"Men should not seek to be causes; their proportion is lost. They are not meant to be so big or so small," Ruth volunteered.

"The struggle is for intellectual freedom," Wen said. Mix had the plane at takeoff speed and was off the runway and into the air. The engines' sound roared over his words, but he knew Ruth heard them. She put up her arm and let it drop as a gesture dismissing Wen's lofty notion.

"Are you a genius, Wen Wilson?" Ruth observed the man's face. He was punished for being one; he had been persecuted for being too keen about the events of his era. Would he deny his grand title? He shifted his weight from one leg to the other in a stand. Would he answer her?

"I'm recording; I'm only witnessing what I've seen. I don't know what that makes me. Don't you finally count me a fool; you've gone this far with me." His eyes were almost wet, glistening with tears. "I'm tired too," Wen said. "Very tired; of course, you've experienced much of the strain of my activism," he said.

That seemed true enough to Ruth. At least, Wen could be humble at right moments. That was part of his draw, appreciating others in their down moods. His words were sustaining again, and Christmas came and went without fanfare. There was colorful wrapping paper. It was festive with glossy ribbons. She received a small jewelry box from Wen and Connie Mae. Alex gave her a carat plus diamond ring, a bit late for engagement, but she liked the glitzy stone. It made her feel younger than her years. She gave Wen and Alex hard covers of Victor Hugo's *Les Miserables*. The babies, all the babies, including Hugh, were given toys. Connie Mae received a much awaited Chinese cookbook; she thought the food was too American at the farm. But the move took precedent in everyone's minds; it made the idea of gift-giving seem insignificant; what could be taken? What would have to be left behind? Ruth even skipped church, the holiday service, because she didn't want the memory of 20 years of Christmases. The New Year, this year, was truly out with the old, the good old, too.

On New Year's Eve day, Ruth sipped bourbon from a plain glass and sat in her library in front of an overseas-sized trunk, packing favorite titles. Unselected books would be moved at a later date. Ruth telephoned Billy Buzzy, and the indulgent playboy nephew would supervise closing down the farming operation, along with David Paul. Billy heartily gave Ruth his best wishes about her marriage and showed no surprise that a husband wouldn't want the burdensome cattle business. Billy lauded what he perceived as a step up in the world, a residence in Switzerland. Explaining an apparent sudden departure was easier than she had ever imagined, maybe too easy, but Ruth was contented today. She stashed *Jane Eyre* into her suitcase and Whitman's collected poems, T.S Eliot's *Four Quartets.* This was how farming ended, with poetry and classic novels!

Alex, Ray, and Lester were bringing Jason home from the hospital today. Jason was allowed to leave the country upon special conditions set by the district attorney. A victim was unclear in the case, and vigilante justice played a role in possibly dropping charges against the younger Piny. Ruth heard Hugh's galloping across the hardwood floors. She tuned into the twins' crying, a wail which she could usually block out. Ruth was at peace with her decision to leave Missouri and the community she once loved. She was calm. Connie Mae entered and sat on the edge of the sofa. Ruth poured her a glass of liquor. She accepted, even though it was early in the afternoon, and there was much work to be done.

"You can learn to ski," Ruth said. Connie Mae was skeptical, and Ruth recalled that she was afraid of toboggan rides on steep white winter hills. The older woman wasn't sure what to say to the busy mother about her future. She packed books faster now, in obvious quiet.

"Wen said that you were faulting him for closing the farm. Ruth, you never said that you didn't want us here. You never once said it, or we would have left," Connie Mae was concerned.

"I'm not blaming, meaning I'm not mad, you're close as family to me." She patted the woman's knee as she walked past. Ruth picked up Phil Boxer's Bible and stuffed it under wind jackets. She would mail it to Phil's forwarding address once she settled in Bern. "I wonder if you ever regret the difficulties of being married to Wen. Why, there's worry, always plenty of worry," Ruth said, noting Connie was shocked at her words.

"Well no," Connie Mae replied. "Wen, though I don't know his thinking or work as I could, is mine. I know he could've done better than a woman like me. He's been everything important. You know, I've never had education, and well, I'm glad he married me. There's an argument once and a while, but we care for each other," Connie said.

"Before he came here, 'importance' was getting the cattle to higher ground during flash floods. I liked farming, a simpler life. Heavens, I love books but am no brain. Don't take any of this wrong; Wen is dear to me. I'm just not one ready for complexity on a 24-hour basis. I'm a farm girl gone to city, gone to school, but farming is in my blood." Connie seemed to sympathize with her words. She knew what Ruth meant.

"Now is not for us to pick through every qualm and misgiving. We must face this coming newness as an adventure, as full of possibilities for the better." She was losing Connie Mae's attention; Connie was interested that no one in the house should be upset at Wen. "I'm okay with Wen," Ruth said so that Connie Mae could return to twins' and their constant needs. The young woman squeezed Ruth's hand and could resume her chores.

After Connie left the room, Ruth considered moving the entire library. She didn't want digital versions of the classics. She wanted 'hard copy' as a staff writer at the local newspaper said. She wanted stubborn and resolved objects, fixtures packed with living words. A library's stacked books nudged her and reminded her of their permanent worth, value without violence or vigilante methods. She applauded herself for fine organization skill too.

Young men crowded into her open living room. A hefty turkey was in the oven for New Year's Day. Ruth beat the thickening gravy and made sure that there were plenty of potatoes for her adopted family. Mix was flying Jason, Lester, and Ray to New York City, where they would be given travel-ready identities and then would fly onto Bern. Lester and Ray were kept on as makeshift nurses and helpers for Jason, who was still recuperating from injuries.

Next, Wen and his family would be moved. Finally, Mix would join Ruth and Alex for a final journey to Switzerland. Ruth grieved leaving David Paul and Lilly. David was now a dependable and mature young man. He had stayed with and cared for her through tough times. Chatter reached a crescendo after dinner, and for once, Ruth and Connie let the dirty plates sit while the group enjoyed each other's company in light of pending loss. It seemed Ruth had forfeited one community for the richness and loyalty of another. It was no bad deal. She wished she had made a cherry cobbler instead of fawning over leather volumes.

Today, the dessert seemed as significant as anything she imagined about texts. She would never be able to erase the many mundane aspects of a farmer woman's life. She loved to feed people. The babies bawled. Wen sang Van Morrison, revealing both a singer's name and a talent. Alex tapped his foot. Mix giggled. The babies bawled. Hugh hugged Connie Mae. Tomorrow, the room would be busy in a different way, but tonight was a blessing from wise, sensible angels.

About the Author

Mattie McClane is an American novelist, poet, and journalist. She is the second and youngest daughter born to James L. and Shirlie I. Myers in Moline, Illinois. Her father was a commercial artist and her mother worked as a secretary.

McClane's earliest education was in the Catholic schools. Her experience with their teachings deeply affected her. At a young age, she became aware of gender inequality. She credits her early religious instruction for making her think about "all kinds of truths and ethical matters."

McClane's parents divorced when she was eight years old. Her mother remarried attorney John G. Ames and the new couple moved to a house beside the Rock River. The river centrally figures in McClane's creative imagination.

She describes her childhood as being "extraordinarily free and close to nature."

McClane moved to Colorado and married John Kaiser in 1979 in Aurora, just East of Denver.

They then moved to Bettendorf, Iowa, where they had three children. John worked as a chemist. Mattie became interested in politics, joining the local League of Women Voters. According to McClane, she spent her 20s "caring for young children and working for good government."

She graduated from Augustana College with a B.A. degree in the Humanities. She began writing a political column for Quad-Cities Online and Small Newspaper Group, based in Illinois.

Her family moved to Louisville, Kentucky where she continued with her journalism and then earned an M.A. in English from the University of Louisville. Critically acclaimed author Sena Jeter Naslund directed her first creative thesis, "Unbuttoning Light and Other Stories," which was later published in a collection.

She was accepted to the University of North Carolina at Wilmington's M.F.A. in Creative Writing Program, where she wrote the short novel *Night Ship*, working under the tutelage of Pulitzer Prize winning author Alison Lurie. McClane studied with Dennis Sampson in poetry also. She graduated in 1999.

She would write a column for the *High Point Enterprise* in North Carolina. She would later write for the *News and Observer*. McClane has regularly published commentary for over 25 years.

Mattie McClane is the author of *Night Ship: A Voyage of Discovery* (2003, 2017), *River Hymn: Essays Evangelical and Political* (2004), *Wen Wilson* (2009, 2022), *Unbuttoning Light: The Collected Short Stories of Mattie McClane* (2012), *Now Time* (2013), *Stations of the Cross* (2016), *The Mother Word: An Exploration of the Visual* (2017), *Simeon's Canticle* (2018), *The Magnificent Light of Morning* (2021), *To Free the Sisters of Mary* (2022).

She lives in North Carolina.